LOS MONSTRUOS

Felice and the Wailing Woman

LOS MONSTRUOS

Felice and the Wailing Woman

. . . .

BY DIANA LÓPEZ

Kokila

KOKILA
An imprint of Penguin Random House LLC, New York

First published in the United States of America by Kokila,
an imprint of Penguin Random House LLC, 2023

Copyright © 2023 by Diana López

Visit us online at penguinrandomhouse.com.

Library of Congress Cataloging-in-Publication Data

Names: López, Diana, author.
Title: Felice and the wailing woman / by Diana López.
Description: New York : Kokila, 2023. | Series: Los monstruos ; 1
Audience: Ages 8-12. | Audience: Grades 4-6.
Summary: "The twelve-year-old daughter of La Llorona vows to free her mother and
reverse the curses that have plagued the magical town of Tres Leches"—Provided by publisher.
Identifiers: LCCN 2022028552 (print) | LCCN 2022028553 (ebook) |
ISBN 9780593326497 (hardcover) | ISBN 9780593326510 (ebook)
Subjects: CYAC: Llorona (Legendary character)—Fiction. | Blessing and
cursing—Fiction. | Fear—Fiction. | Mothers—Fiction. | Magic—Fiction. | LCGFT: Novels.
Classification: LCC PZ7.L876352 Fe 2023 (print) | LCC PZ7.L876352 (ebook) | DDC [Fic]—dc23
LC record available at https://lccn.loc.gov/2022028552
LC ebook record available at https://lccn.loc.gov/2022028553

Printed in the United States of America

ISBN 9780593326497

1st Printing
LSCH

This book was edited by Joanna Cárdenas, copyedited by Diane João, proofread by Jacqueline Hornberger,
and designed by Jasmin Rubero. The production was supervised by Tabitha Dulla, Nicole Kiser,
Ariela Rudy Zaltzman, and Hansini Weedagama.

Text set in Anglecia Pro Text

For Steban, Seth, and Deven

PROLOGUE

TODAY, THE STUDENTS OF Tres Leches Middle School in Tejas would rather eat dirt than go on a field trip. *This* field trip, to be exact. They'd rather stay inside and take pop quizzes. They'd rather eat raw broccoli for lunch and do 1,153 jumping jacks for PE. Instead, they move slowly, double-knotting their shoelaces and topping off their water bottles as Mr. Tercero hurries them along. "¡Ándenle!" he says.

They've heard of other schools in other towns with field trips to museums, or firehouses, or historic sites like the Alamo. They've heard that instead of hiking to their destinations, the students travel by bus. They've even heard—and this one's hard to believe—that the field trips often include tour guides who know everything and then some, and gift shops—yes, gift shops!—where visitors can buy postcards or refrigerator magnets or tiny spoons. But for the pobrecitos of Tres Leches, there were no buses, tour guides, or gift shops. They went to only three places, and they went to these places every year—El Camarón Dance Hall & Arcade in the fall, the mud expanse in the winter, and La Llorona Park in the spring. The "park" part was always said tongue-in-cheek, and if anyone knew what the opposite of a park was, they would have used that word instead.

"Come on. Let's go!" Ms. Peters calls out. And so the students start their trek, not bothering to look around or make jokes. They pass the playground and the library and the vacant lot. They march right out of town, crossing the soon-to-be bluebonnet field and a small, dark forest, and on the other side of it, a clearing of mostly dead grass. They gulp warm water from their bottles and swat at mosquitoes, the humid air thick around them, until finally arriving at a wooden marker—like a tombstone—nearly hidden by webs and vines.

"Stop!" Mr. Tercero demands. The students freeze, not daring to go farther. The teachers pull out hedge shears and pruners, and they start cutting away, little by little revealing a sign.

BEWARE THE RIVER,
FOR HERE HAUNTS LA LLORONA.
IN LIFE, SHE WAS A FOOL FOR LOVE.
THEN SHE DROWNED HER CHILDREN OUT OF SPITE,
AND NOW HER GHOST WANTS TO DROWN YOU, TOO.

The teachers and the students take a moment to read. Some of the braver souls speak the words aloud, while others can only manage to mouth them silently.

Then the principal, Ms. Cavasos, says, "Any volunteers?" After a moment of silence, she asks again, this time with a "Hmm?"

The students look at their double-knotted shoelaces and the burrs clinging to their socks.

"Very well, then," Ms. Cavasos says, opening a bag. One by one, the students utter a prayer and reach in. They pull out folded bits of paper. "Don't look till I say," Ms. Cavasos reminds them. The last student reaches into the bag. She has no choice but to take the remaining paper. At that, the principal says, "Okay. You can look now."

The students unfold the papers, most sighing with relief except for Ignacio, whose paper is marked with an X. The poor boy shivers and asks his friends, "Want to trade? Want to trade?" but no one accepts the offer.

Ms. Cavasos puts a hand on his shoulder. "You're a daring boy," she assures him, but he looks scared.

Then Coach steps forward with a rope. He ties one end around Ignacio's waist, and because Coach is strong and makes a good anchor, he ties the other end around his own waist.

"It's time to step forward," Ms. Cavasos tells Ignacio. "Report what you hear and what you feel. You're our hero today. Your friends"—she waves an arm at them—"they need to be reminded."

Ignacio gulps.

"And when we return to town, you'll be rewarded with a delicious slice of tres leches cake," she adds.

This is usually a strong motivation, but not today. Instead, Ignacio looks back at his friends as if to ask for help. They can only nod to urge him forward.

Ignacio turns toward the river. He clenches his fists, closes his eyes, and takes one step and then another. About ten steps in, he moans. "Oh!" he cries. "I hear La Llorona! She's crying! It's so terrible!"

"What is she saying?" Ms. Peters wants to know.

"She's calling for her children. She wants her children," Ignacio answers. "She's calling for me. *I'm* her child. I need to go to her!"

"Cover your ears!" his friends tell him. "Turn back!"

"But she needs me!" Ignacio says with urgency.

He runs forward, and suddenly the rope goes taut. Coach digs his heels in the dirt to hold Ignacio back, but it works only for a few seconds.

"Quick! I need help," Coach calls.

Mr. Tercero and five or six students grab the rope for an intense tug-of-war.

It shouldn't be possible for one small boy like Ignacio to hold them off, but the dreadful lure of La Llorona's spell is unparalleled.

"Pull!" Coach shouts, and the rope moves a little. "Pull!" he shouts again.

Coach, Mr. Tercero, and the students pull, using the full force of their muscles and will. Their hands get sweaty, and their arms and legs start to shake, but inch by inch, they manage to reel Ignacio in. When he's on the safe side of the sign, everyone drops to the ground, exhausted. They ask for their water bottles, some for drinking and others for pouring the water over their heads.

After a stunned moment, Ignacio unties the rope, rubs at his belly, and starts to sob. "I wanted to go to her, even though her cries were like a nightmare. Why did I want to go to her? She would have drowned me. I knew she wanted to drown me, and I *still* wanted to go."

Ms. Cavasos nods knowingly. "That's the curse of La Llorona. She tricks you into thinking you're her child, and when she sees that you're not ... well, let's just say her rage takes over." Then, turning to the group, she says, "You must never go past this sign, for if you do, you will hear La Llorona's cries and feel compelled to approach the river, where she'll grab you and—"

She stops midsentence. The students nod because they all know what will happen next. They've been coming to La Llorona "Park" every year since kindergarten, and they'll keep coming till they graduate from high school, because you could never hear it enough: *Beware the river, beware the river, beware ...*

CAN'T SLEEP, FELICE?

EVERY FEAR GETS A special word. Fear of heights? *Acrophobia.* Fear of the dark? *Nyctophobia.* Fear of flying in an airplane or riding in a car? *Aerophobia* and *amaxophobia.* These fears make sense, since there might be danger involved, but some people fear non-dangerous things, too, like the color white (*leukophobia*) or the number eight (*octophobia*). There are words for people who fear knees, flowers, or ferns, and for those who fear clocks, books, or beards. But even when a fear doesn't have a special word, it's easy to make one up—like *lampophobia* for fear of lampshades or *crinklephobia* for fear of crinkly things.

Me? I fear water—lakes, oceans, rivers, and rain. Especially rain. How can people clap for it, dance in it, or write cheery songs like "Singin' in the Rain" and "Raindrops Keep Fallin' on My Head"? The sound of it pattering on the roof, the sheets of it running down the windows, the V-shaped waves formed by cars in flooded streets—these make my teeth clatter, my throat tighten, and my hands and feet go cold as my blood skedaddles from fear.

And right now, it's raining! That's why I'm awake even though it's after midnight.

I go down the hall, knock on Uncle Clem's door. It's just us. He's been taking care of me since I was a baby.

"Uncle Clem?" I call softly because I don't want to startle him.

I hear movement. Then he's at the door, rubbing sleep from his eyes.

"Can't sleep, Felice?" he asks, and I don't have to admit that I'm afraid because he already knows. "Follow me," he says, so I do, straight to the kitchen. He turns on the light, and I squint in the sudden brightness. Now it's *my* turn to rub my eyes.

"I need to rest," I say. "Big day tomorrow. But I can't stop worrying about the rain."

He scratches his head, thinking. "We'll just have to disguise it."

"How do we do that?" I ask.

"By finding something that sounds like rain but isn't." He thinks some more. "Tap dancing? Drumming? Shaking the maracas?"

We don't have tap dance shoes or drums, but the maracas are somewhere in this house. I start opening junk drawers, but then I catch Uncle Clem smiling. He goes to the pantry and takes out the Jiffy Pop. Of course! It's a great idea! He turns on the gas stove and holds the pan over the flame. First there's one pop, then two, then a rapid fire of pops, louder than the rain and much more delicious. We eat the popcorn, and then we make more because it's still raining, but it's not so terrifying any-more, not with the buttery goodness of popcorn, the saltiness that's best washed down with an ice-cold Topo Chico.

"Hear that?" Uncle Clem asks.

I listen. Nothing. "The rain stopped!"

"It sure did, and nothing bad happened. You're okay. I'm okay. We didn't even lose power."

"I know. It's just—"

He doesn't let me finish my thought. "No need to remember that terrible night. Let's try to get some sleep now, okay?"

I nod, head back to my room, and pretend I'm fine, but I'm not. The rain might have stopped, but my fear is still with me. It's got a special word, too, *aquaphobia*: the fear of water. The reason I suffer from it is because water's what took most of my family and what almost took me.

I was a baby when it happened, so I don't have specific memories, just nightmares sometimes. When I want to remember the details, I unfold a newspaper article: MOTHER AND SONS DROWN WHILE CROSSING RIVER, INFANT DAUGHTER RESCUED BY UNCLE. I'm the infant daughter, and

Uncle Clem is the one who rescued me. He never talks about "the event"; he says it's better to pretend it didn't happen. But it *did* happen. That night at the river is a part of me.

I can't remember the night my family drowned, but I do have nightmares of my mother crying for her children, which means she's crying for me.

HE WAS THE MAKER
OF THINGS THAT CRACK

THE NEXT DAY IS the Friday before spring break. I
can't wait to get out of school, but when the dismissal
bell rings, I don't go home right away. First, I stop at Mrs.
Hart's house, checking her mailbox before making my
way to her door. She uses a walker and really struggles
to get down the porch stairs. That's why I grab the mail
for her.

"I won't be here next week," I say, "but I'll return the
week after."

She hands me a little bag. "You're such a sweetie. I
saw this at the store and remembered how much you
like art. It's just a little token of my appreciation."

I peek inside—a tray of watercolors.

"Thank you, Mrs. Hart." I put the tray in my purse
even though I'll never open it because . . . well . . . they're
*water*colors.

Then I walk along Schanen Trail because there's
a lot to see—basketball games, bike riders, and pretty

flowers—and everything's fine until a dog starts growling. It's Cammy, a Chihuahua. She's always getting loose and terrorizing the neighborhood. Even now she bares her teeth and growls.

"Whoa, Cammy! It's me, Felice."

She adds a few barks to her growling. Cammy's never bitten anyone as far as I know, but she sure likes to scare people. Luckily, Uncle Clem gave me good advice one day. He said, *You can calm the meanest dog if you throw him a biscuit.* For that reason, I keep Milk-Bones in my purse. I toss one to Cammy, who sniffs it before gobbling it up. Now she's wagging her tail, the dog version of a smile. I like making people and puppies happy. That's why I carry a happy face emoji purse. It's round and yellow, with glittery heart eyes and … yup! … a giant smile.

After Cammy runs off, I head to my street, Sunlight Drive. I take a moment to note the wet sidewalks. Then I start zigzagging, my path like a shoelace. I know it's dangerous to cross the street so many times, but how else can I avoid the sprinklers?

When I get to my house, there's a strange car parked in front. No, not a car—a truck—but not exactly a truck, either. Its tires are almost as tall as my front door, so I'm actually looking *under* the truck instead of *at* it. I can see rods, coils, axles, and a whole tangle of metal things. The sun visor above the windshield is shaped like a pair of angry brows. There's a row of spikes along the roof of the cab, and two nostril-shaped openings on the hood. The front grille is a snarling mouth with fangs, and the body of the truck is painted red with orange flames forming the words *El Cucuy*, the name of the scariest *monstruo* from all our bedtime stories.

I gulp with fear when I see this truck named after a monster, but then I shake it off. How silly of me. Everyone knows monsters aren't real.

I step inside the house. "Hello!" I call.

"¡Hola!" I hear. Uncle Clem always says *hello* and *goodbye* in Spanish—*hola, buenos días, vaya con Dios*—but for almost everything else, he speaks English.

I find him in the dining room, but he's not alone. We have a visitor, probably the owner of the monster truck. He's a skinny man who looks familiar even though I'm sure we've never met. He's wearing jeans and a light blue guayabera, only it's short, barely covering his belt and its giant silver buckle with the word *Mayor* on it. He's got a long braid, and his face is weathered from too much time in the sun.

"Hello?" I say, this time a question.

Uncle Clem waves me in. "Felice, meet—"

"What an honor!" our visitor says, turning to shake my hand, then kissing it, then twirling me under his arm as if we're dancing. When he finally lets go, I'm dizzy. "Look at you! *Look* at you!" he says. "You're as beautiful as your mother. You have the same long black hair and big brown eyes."

"You knew my mother?"

"Of course I knew her!"

"This is Reynaldo, from Tres Leches," Uncle Clem explains.

That's who he is. There are pictures of him, a younger version, in our photo albums.

"Growing up, we were best friends," my uncle adds.

"*Are* best friends," Reynaldo corrects. "Todavía. Even though we haven't seen each other in years."

My uncle nods. He's shared a couple of stories about Reynaldo, how he once fixed a radiator with a nail file and how he spent a whole year collecting boxes so he could build a giant maze for a festival.

Reynaldo turns to my uncle. "Remember, my friend, when you made that Halloween piñata?"

"In the shape of a giant spider."

"Yes! And instead of dulces inside, it had—"

"Spiders!" My uncle laughs.

Reynaldo's laughing, too. "You weren't subtle. That's for sure."

My uncle, a prankster? I never imagined it.

"Why would you put spiders inside a piñata?" I ask.

"It was a customer's request," he says. "It took me days to capture them."

"He was climbing into every attic"—Reynaldo giggles—"crawling beneath every house, and searching every abandoned storage shed."

I try to picture my uncle doing these things, being creative this way. Uncle Clem is a copy editor, a stickler for details and correctness. His customers don't ask for piñatas. They send him documents and deadlines.

"What did you do before you were a copy editor?" I ask him, realizing that I've never wondered before.

Reynaldo responds instead. "Your uncle was the greatest cracksman in Tres Leches County." And before I can ask, he explains, "He was a maker of things that crack."

"Like the piñatas?" I guess.

"And cascarones, piggy banks, and crispy taco shells."

I can't believe this! In all these years, Uncle Clem has never made any of those things. He's never allowed piñatas for birthdays or confetti eggs for Easter. He puts his spare change in a shoebox. And he always insists on *soft* tacos.

"In fact," Reynaldo goes on, "one of the reasons I'm here is to convince your uncle to return as our cracksman." He straightens up as if to make a speech. "Without piñatas and cascarones, there is no joy. Without piggy banks, there is no wealth. And without crispy taco shells, there . . . there . . . there are no crispy tacos."

"It sounds like they need you," I say to my uncle.

"Well, I like the job I have right now," he answers.

Reynaldo scoffs. I almost do, too. Being a cracksman sounds a lot more interesting than being a copy editor.

Uncle Clem turns to his friend. "So why else are you here? You said that was one reason, but what's the other?"

"Alegra," Reynaldo says.

When I hear this, I can't contain my excitement. Alegra was my mother's name.

"Tell me about her," I urge Reynaldo. "Tell me *everything*."

"Oh, she was beautiful." He closes his eyes a moment. If only I could jump into his imagination, see his memories for myself. "She was very graceful when she walked. Looked like she was floating."

"Like an angel?" I say.

"Yes, an angel. Why do you ask? Did I say she floated like a ghost?"

"No."

"Oh, thank goodness. My words run faster than my brain sometimes, and my brain . . . it runs very fast, so you can imagine how much faster my words can be."

It's true. Even now, I'm trying to process what he's saying.

"What was my mom's favorite recipe?" I want to know. "What books did she read? Did she like to draw? Did you know Gustavo and Henry, my brothers? What were they like?"

"Stop pestering our guest," Uncle Clem says.

"But I want details. You're always telling me how nice and smart Mom was, but—"

"Well," Reynaldo interrupts, "I guess you could say she was *mostly* nice, and I guess you could say she had a *slightly*-above-average level of intelligence."

My uncle raises an eyebrow and gives Reynaldo a warning glance.

"What I mean," Reynaldo rushes to explain, "is that someone can be nice but also mean. Wise but also foolish. Responsible but also irresponsible. Corporeal but also—"

"I think she understands," Uncle Clem says, shaking his head at his friend's dramatic way of presenting things.

"So just tell me the good parts," I say to Reynaldo. "Knowing half the story is better than knowing nothing at all."

"She makes a good point," Reynaldo says. "She should meet her mother."

"Meet her?" I repeat.

"Figuratively speaking," Uncle Clem is quick to say.

"Yes, yes. Figuratively." Reynaldo uses air quotes for the last word.

Uncle Clem puts his hands on my shoulders and turns me around. "But not right now, mija. Reynaldo and I have some important things to discuss about our family. So go to your room and do your homework."

"I don't have any homework. It's spring break."

"Then read a book or draw a picture. Give the grown-ups some privacy."

"But I'm practically a grown-up already!"

He crosses his arms. "¿Perdón?"

I stop protesting because he's switched to Spanish, which means he's getting impatient. Before leaving, I glance back. Reynaldo shrugs as if apologizing.

As I head to my room, Uncle Clem calls, "And shut the door behind you."

I do as he says, and the wind from the closing door flutters the pages of my calendar. Every year, Uncle Clem buys me a calendar that features art. One year, it had Navajo tapestries. Another year, Frida Kahlo's art. And this year, Monet's. He painted landscapes, but all his colors and shapes blur together.

I go to my desk. There are a few library books, a sketch pad, and coffee cups with pencils, chalk, and pastels. I glance at my bed, at the space between the mattress and the box spring, where I hide sketches of my mother.

Why won't Uncle Clem let me hear the conversation about my family, especially when I already know that they drowned? As for my father, he was already married when he met my mom, and eventually he left her to be with his wife. He was more than happy to let Uncle Clem have custody of me after my mom died. My father sends child-support checks and cards on special occasions, but

I never see him. I should be sad about this, but in my mind, he doesn't really matter. Uncle Clem's my real dad, if you ask me. That's why I don't ask for stories about my father. But the others—my mom and brothers? I know how they died; shouldn't I also know how they lived? Seems like Reynaldo wants to tell me a whole lot more than Uncle Clem ever has.

Maybe . . . maybe that's what their secret discussion is about. Very carefully, I open my bedroom door, tiptoe into the hallway, and stop just out of sight. If it's *my* family they're talking about and anyone has a right to know what they're saying, it's me.

¡AYÚDAME!

AS I EAVESDROP ON Uncle Clem and Reynaldo, I pretend to be an investigator or an operative for the CIA by holding my breath and standing very, very still.

"So, Bonita's still up to her old tricks, is she?" Uncle Clem says.

"Old tricks and new," Reynaldo answers.

"I'm just glad it's not my problem anymore. Besides, Tres Leches is in good hands with you as the mayor."

"I won't be *staying* mayor if I can't fix the river. That was the whole point of my campaign. I promised to make it safe so people could swim again and go tubing."

I guess the river's been off-limits ever since my family drowned.

"You shouldn't make promises you can't keep," Uncle Clem says.

"But Bonita's making the same promises, and she has ways to keep them. Supernatural ways. Please, Clem, come home. I'm running out of time. Our last debate is in a few days and the election's the day after that."

"Like I said, amigo. I need to stay here, where Felice and I are safe. Tres Leches is not my problem anymore."

There's a moment of silence, and then Reynaldo's voice gets desperate. "What about your sister? Isn't she your problem?"

How can my mother be a problem when she died so long ago?

I hear my uncle's loud sigh. "My sister's dead."

Reynaldo gives a "ha!" and then: "Is that what you tell yourself?"

"Yes, because it's the truth."

"Well, there are many ways to be dead," Reynaldo says, "and many ways to be alive. Sometimes death looks like life and life looks like death. Sometimes people get stuck—"

"No more riddles, Reynaldo! I'm sorry for the people of Tres Leches, but I left all that behind. I have a new life now—a job, a house, and Felice. I have to protect her. She's all that matters to me."

"That's why she deserves to know the truth."

Yes, I deserve to know the truth! I inch forward a bit, hoping to hear more, but Uncle Clem ends the conversation. "I heard you out like I promised, but there's nothing I can do. It's time for you to leave, my friend. A mayor shouldn't be away for so long." I hear the creaky front door open. First there's silence, then footsteps—Reynaldo's, I'm guessing.

"I know it's a big decision," Reynaldo says, his voice getting fainter as he walks outside. "Sleep on it. I'll be at the taquería on Everhart at seven in the morning. You and Felice can join me. Together we can help your sister and make the river safe again."

"I won't be changing my mind," Uncle Clem answers.

"You might."

"I won't."

Reynaldo's still talking, but I can't make out the words.

The next thing I hear is Uncle Clem calling out, "¡Mucho cuidado!"

That's when I run from my hiding place, rushing past my uncle. "Wait! Wait!" I shout, but the monster truck is already down the street. I wave my arms to get Reynaldo's attention, but he doesn't see me. The truck turns a corner. I can hear the loud growl of its engine, but then it fades away. It's just my street now, with the same cars in the driveways, the same plants in the yards, the same dogs barking from behind fences—everything the same but also different because now I'm wondering if the cars are messy or neat on the inside and who planted the flowers and how old the barking dogs are. I have a million questions suddenly, but none as important as the questions about my family.

Uncle Clem's on the front porch, watching me. I march up the steps, cross my arms. "What was Reynaldo talking about?" I ask. "Why did he keep saying that my mother needs you?"

"He's always been a little eccentric," Uncle Clem says.

That's a response, not an answer. I know because I do the same thing when I'm trying to avoid a question. Uncle Clem calls me on it every time, so I throw it back at him. "That's a response, not an answer."

He winces. Then he reaches for the armrest of our porch swing, steadying it as he sits down.

"Is Mom still alive? Yes or no?"

"She drowned, mija."

I stand in front of him, my shadow darkening his face.

"Yes or no? Is she still alive?"

He won't answer directly. "One day, your mother slipped a note beneath the door to my shop. I didn't notice it right away. I was too busy working. Why was I working so hard? If only ... if only ..." His thoughts trail off for a bit—his face gloomy and dark like a window covered in mud—but soon he's back to his story. "The note said she was taking you and your brothers to meet your dad on the other side of the river. There were no roads to where he was, so I figured I could catch her if I ran. But the rain slowed me down because I kept slipping. Then, as I got closer to the river, I heard the screams. She was already drowning when I reached her."

Uncle Clem wipes his eyes. I should give him a hug, but I won't because he still hasn't answered my question.

"Is she alive?"

He shakes his head. "She drowned, mija. You know this. You know how I ran along the banks of the river, yelling at her to grab at branches, at anything, but she wouldn't let you go. Then one of your brothers screamed for her. He was so scared. And when your mother scrambled for him, she lost hold of you. She tried reaching for you again. She tried reaching for your brothers. She just couldn't. She couldn't save you and your brothers and herself. She couldn't save anyone. I raced down the bank, trying to get ahead, to grab all of you, but you're the only one I managed to pull out."

"So you saw them drown?"

"The river took them away."

"That's not an answer, Uncle Clem! Why can't you be honest with me? I need to know what happened."

"I'm so glad I saved you," Uncle Clem goes on. "But I wish I'd done more. If only I had been strong enough and fast enough. If only I had thought to ask others to join me. Why did I go alone? I cringed when the newspaper called me a hero, because I wasn't, not in my mind.

"After the drowning, I couldn't go back to working in my shop. How could I make colorful piñatas when my whole life felt gray? I closed the curtains and sat in the dark, moving only when you needed attention. The townspeople stayed away from us just as they stayed away from Alegra after your father left. Only Reynaldo, my one true friend, would call, but I wouldn't answer. I couldn't.

"Then, one day, he stood on the other side of the door and said, 'Your sister became La Llorona, always crying. Are you, mi amigo, destined to be El Llorón?' And at that moment, you wailed. You didn't need a diaper change. You weren't hungry. The wailing came from a broken heart. I tried rocking you and singing, but you wouldn't calm down. That's when I realized that you'd be cursed with sadness if we stayed in Tres Leches. That's when I grabbed our things and moved us away."

"Uncle Clem." I speak softly, trying my best to hold back tears. "Why is Reynaldo saying that my mother needs your help? Did she and my brothers really drown? Did you see it happen?"

"I didn't see it, mija. The river took them away. They're gone. They're gone forever. I know your mother. She would never leave her children. If she were alive, she'd be with you."

"But maybe she doesn't know where I am." My voice catches in my throat because I'm losing my fight against the tears.

Uncle Clem stands up. He hugs me, kisses the top of my head. His chest trembles as he sobs. He really *is* a cracksman, and the thing that's cracking is his heart.

"This is why I don't like to talk about it," he reminds me. "It's too painful. We can't change the past. The best way to honor the memory of our family is to be happy and helpful and kind, to live good lives."

It's wise advice, but it doesn't comfort me. We step back into the house. I wash my face and blow my nose. I try to pretend that things are normal. Uncle Clem asks about my day at school. He suggests activities for spring break. He cooks dinner. The whole time, I'm having two conversations—one where my *mouth* is speaking, answering his questions, and another where my *brain* is speaking, asking questions.

In my room again, I touch the library books and art supplies on my desk, but I'm not interested in reading or drawing. I take my happy face emoji purse and turn it upside down so it's frowning. I glance at my bed. Then I squeeze my hand between the mattress and box spring to pull out the sketch pad with pictures of my mother. Sometimes I draw her lying in the grasslands. She's hard to see because her hair is long; it covers her robe. But she's there—black strands in the golden grass. In another sketch, she's brushing her hair over her face. Her wrists have giant knobs, and the wrinkles on her finger joints look like screaming mouths. Once, I drew her as a weeping willow—the trunk, her body; the branches, her arms; her face covered by strings of leaves. Often, I just draw her hands—never in prayer or quietly folded on her lap. They're usually reaching for something, something off the page—my brothers? me?—or they're in front of her face as if she's blocking blows. Sometimes I hide words in the lines of her palms—*¡Ayúdame!* and *¡Mis hijos!* and *¿Dónde están?* I don't speak much Spanish, but when I dream of her, these are the words I hear.

YOU'VE NEVER TASTED THIS MOST DELICIOUS DESSERT?

EARLY THE NEXT MORNING, I dump out books from my backpack and stuff a toothbrush, colored pencils, and a sketch pad inside. I loop the happy face emoji purse over my shoulder and take the newspaper article about my family, neatly folding it and slipping it in my pocket. Then I tiptoe through the house, wincing every time the floor creaks. I open the front door, one inch at a time, and when I finally step through, I shut it inch by inch again. It clicks closed. I wait a full minute, praying that my uncle is still asleep. When I'm convinced, I step off the porch. "Bye, Uncle Clem," I whisper. Then I tuck a note beneath his windshield wiper. I'm sure he'll go to his car when he discovers I'm missing, and that's when he'll see where I've gone.

The taquería where Reynaldo waits is walking distance from my house, so I head in that direction. Every passing car startles me because I've never run away before, and I can't stop imagining search parties and Amber Alerts even though I just left.

It's humid, so by the time I reach Everhart, my shirt is damp and my bangs are stuck to my forehead. I glance at my watch. It's almost seven, and I still have to walk past the car wash and gas station and Sandcastle Apartments. I hurry, worried that I'm late. Will Reynaldo still be there? What if I imagined the whole thing or got the details wrong? I was eavesdropping from behind a wall. Maybe I didn't hear correctly.

Finally, I see the taquería, and in the parking lot— taking up three spaces!—is Reynaldo's monster truck. At first I'm excited—I *did* get the details right—but then my inner voice starts screaming: *Don't talk to strangers! Don't hitchhike!* and *Beware of El Cucuy!* But Reynaldo's not a stranger, not really. I might not know him, but I know *of* him, been hearing stories my whole life. And I'm not really hitchhiking, because that would mean standing on the side of the road and sticking out my thumb till someone stops. As for El Cucuy? It's a monster truck, not a real monster.

I step into the restaurant, and Reynaldo immediately sees me. He stands and pulls out a chair. "Sit, sit," he says. Then he snaps to get the waiter's attention, and when the waiter arrives, Reynaldo says, "Get my friend some coffee."

"I don't drink coffee," I say.

"Well then. Would you like tea, soda, hot chocolate, agua de horchata?"

I shake my head.

"Orange juice, grapefruit juice, apple juice, or a kiwi-strawberry blend?"

"All we got is orange juice," the waiter says.

"I'll just have water," I tell the waiter. "And could you put it in a to-go cup with a lid and a straw?" He nods and heads to the kitchen.

"Ah yes," Reynaldo says as he returns to his seat. "Water should have been my first guess. It is the purest of refreshments, the most primal of ingredients, for all life began in the oceans. It is the very life force of—"

"It also drowns people," I say.

He sighs. "Sadly, this is true."

He lifts his coffee cup and blows into it before taking a sip. The waiter returns with my water. He stands there, waiting for our order.

"I'll have a chorizo con huevo taquito," I say.

"And I'll have"—Reynaldo glances at the menu again—"the migas plate."

The waiter writes down our order.

"And for Clemente?" Reynaldo asks. "What will he be ordering?"

"He's still at home," I say. "And he refuses to go to Tres Leches, *ever*. He says my mother is dead, and I need to let it go and move on."

The waiter clears his throat. "Will that be all?" he asks.

Reynaldo nods and waves him away.

Once the waiter's gone, I ask Reynaldo, "So, is she? Is my mother really dead?"

He thinks for a moment, then says, "It depends on how you define death, or better yet, life. If you ask your uncle, she's dead, but if you ask me, she's not."

"But is she literally alive?" I ask, remembering how Uncle Clem had said "figuratively speaking" the day before.

"Yes, yes, quite literally."

I grab a napkin, thinking I'm going to cry from joy now that I know she's alive, but instead, I tear at it because my mom has stayed away all these years. Little pieces fall on my lap, and as I brush them to the floor, I think . . . Is this what my mother did? Brush me aside?

"So where is she? If she loves me, why isn't she with me?"

"She's looking for you, but remember, the last time she saw you was at the river. She believes you're still there."

"She still lives in Tres Leches?"

"Not technically. She's at the river, searching, always searching, and always crying. Some say her tears keep the water flowing."

"Do they still call her La Llorona?"

He lifts an eyebrow, surprised that I know about this.

"Uncle Clem told me the whole town called her La Llorona," I explain.

"They still do," Reynaldo admits. "But in their defense, she cries all the time. She has never stopped."

I imagine my mother crying for twelve years while I've been having a good time laughing, making friends, and learning to draw. I grab another napkin and tear at it again, only this time, I'm not angry about the idea of my mother staying away. I'm angry at Uncle Clem. How could he have kept us apart?

"I want to go to her," I say. "I want to meet her."

Reynaldo's about to respond, but our food arrives. He douses his plate with salsa and digs in. I take a bite of the chorizo taquito, and a little stream of hot grease runs down my arm.

"I'm so pleased you understand," Reynaldo says with his mouth full. "We'll finish breakfast and then, together, we can convince Clemente."

I swallow hard. My uncle will never return to Tres Leches, even if I beg him. Besides, he's been lying to me all these years.

"We can't go back to my uncle," I say. "He'll never understand. He doesn't like me helping people, and obviously this includes my mother. Every time I get a B or C on an assignment because I was helping someone else get an A, every time I run out of money because I gave it to someone who seemed to need it more, every time I let people cut in line at the grocery store or take the last Snickers bar from the candy machine—Uncle Clem gets after me, telling me that I have to watch out for myself first. If we go back to him, he'll send you away, and I'll never meet my mother. Please, Reynaldo. Please! You have to take me with you. I left a note with Uncle Clem, telling him where I am. He can come after me if he wants."

"I'm not sure I should take you anywhere without permission," Reynaldo says.

I know it's good that he doesn't want to do something behind my uncle's back, but right now, being good is keeping me from my mother. "So that's it? We're just going to finish breakfast and then you're taking me home?"

"I'm afraid so. I can't go against my best friend."

I stare at my half-eaten taquito. I'll never meet my mother, I realize. All I ever wanted was to see her, hug her, smell her hair. Some girls might want a mom for big, important things, but I want her for the small things, the everyday things, the things that most daughters forget. How I would love to forget moments with her— not because I don't want to remember but because it would mean that I had so many memories, too many for my giant brain to hold. Mostly, I miss having a mom in my life, especially now when I have so many questions about becoming a woman.

"Fine!" I say to Reynaldo. "If you won't take me and he won't take me, I'll go to the river by myself." As I say this, my pulse starts to race, panic threatening to take over. I force myself to keep from hyperventilating. I don't mention that I'm afraid of water because it'll give him another reason to leave me behind.

"Whoa, whoa, whoa! Wait, wait, wait!" Reynaldo says. "You shouldn't go by yourself. You need someone to protect you. You don't want to get hurt. Not that your mother would hurt you—that's not what I meant at all— but on account of . . . because of . . . well . . . since she's at a dangerous river. Yes! That's what I mean. You need to take precautions. A life buoy and rope, but also a life vest and snorkel. Maybe some flippers. Towels. Definitely towels. And probably some Kleenex, since your mother cries so much and you might cry too when you see her, not from sadness, certainly not *that*, but from joy. Have you ever heard the quote, 'Excessive sorrow laughs; excessive joy weeps'? No? Well, it's a very famous quote. So you'll be crying tears of joy, that's the point I'm making, and for those tears of joy, you'll need Kleenex. And finally, but most importantly, you'll need earplugs to block out the sound."

"You mean to block out the water?"

"Yes, yes. What did I say?" He slaps his cheeks. "Earplugs because water in the ears is most annoying. But in addition to keeping out water, earplugs have the pleasant side effect of keeping out sounds, disturbing sounds that might compel you to jump into the river."

"No sound could ever make me do that."

"Of course not. Forgive me. I get confused. I'm thinking about raccoons and squirrels and a viejita's cat. *They* were compelled." He lifts his coffee cup, then puts it back down, takes his fork, and stabs at his migas. "Besides," he says, "who knows if the river is trickling or gushing? And your mother might be on this side or the other side. It's impossible to predict. She might even be floating *above* the river."

"You mean floating *in* it?"

"Oh yes, of course. That's not what I said?" He shakes his head and slaps his cheeks again.

"If my mother is on the other side, can't I just cross a bridge?" I ask. I'm afraid of bridges, too, since they're often over water, but if I keep looking up and taking deep breaths while I'm on one, I think I can manage.

"We'll cross that bridge when we get to it," Reynaldo says. "But first—"

"So there *is* a bridge?"

"No. No bridge. I was speaking figuratively."

Now I'm shaking my head. I'm so confused. I can't tell the difference between straight talk and riddles.

"Okay, then," I say. "I got it. I need a life vest and some earplugs. Thanks for your advice. Now if you'll excuse me, I'm going to find my mother."

I push back my chair, but he grabs my wrist before I can stand. "No!" he says. "You can't! It's too dangerous!"

"Why? Because of the river? She's my mother. She'll protect me."

"Yes, yes, she's your mother but she's also . . . she's . . ." He takes a deep breath, looks me straight in the eyes, and whispers, "She's your mother, but she's also a ghost."

A ghost? I turn this over and over in my mind, imagining the ghosts of scary stories, how they do things like move furniture, throw books, and flick the light switches. On Halloween, people wear sheets to disguise themselves as ghosts, so that's what I'm imagining—a ghostly white form with two empty circles where the eyes should be. And this form is haunting a house or a school or . . . or . . . or a river. It all makes sense now. No wonder Uncle Clem insists my mother's dead, while Reynaldo is convinced she's alive. She's caught in the in-between space. I know I should be afraid of her, but I'm not. She's still my mother. I love her no matter what, and now that I know she's a ghost, I realize that not only do *I* need *her*, but *she* needs *me*. She's stuck, and I want to help her get *un*stuck.

"Take me with you," I plead. "I don't care if she's a ghost. I still want to meet her."

"But your uncle . . ."

"What about him?" I say because I'm angry. Uncle

Clem wants me to forget about the past even though he knows I'm still trying to understand what happened all those years ago. "How can you say he's your best friend," I ask Reynaldo, "when he never writes, or calls, or visits?"

Reynaldo looks down. He takes a bite of his tortilla, but he isn't chewing with joy anymore. I can tell I hit a nerve, and the last thing I want is to hurt the feelings of the only person who can take me to my mother.

"Do you want to know what my uncle wants?" I say. "More than anything, he wants me to be happy." I hold up my happy face emoji purse for proof. "And I can never be happy till I meet my mother, but I'll never meet her because my uncle wants nothing to do with the town. He won't even order tres leches cake."

Reynaldo's eyes go wide. "You've never tasted this most delicious dessert?"

"Never."

He picks up his butter knife and twirls it absent-mindedly while he thinks. "Perhaps your uncle is over-whelmed by grief. He would not intentionally keep you from your mother. Furthermore, how could he ever in the right state of mind deny *you*, his beloved sobrina, the joy of tres leches cake?"

I see an opening and grab it. "He says that upside-down pineapple cake tastes better."

Shocked, Reynaldo drops the butter knife. He's frozen for a a long time.

"I've decided," he says. "I will take you to the river, where you will finally meet your mother and where you can dry her tears—figuratively speaking—and once the river's safe, I will win the election and everyone will celebrate by eating tres leches cake and tubing down the river."

I brighten up. No way will I ever go tubing down a river, but I can definitely imagine baking and eating tres leches cake with my mom. I want to learn all her recipes.

"You'll take me, then?" I ask Reynaldo.

"Ah yes," he answers. "Soon you will see that our little town is the sweetest place in Tejas, and it'll be even sweeter once you meet your mother."

IT'S MOSTLY A DEAD ZONE
OVER THERE

AT THE MONSTER TRUCK, Reynaldo cups his hands and makes a foothold to give me a lift, but I still have to climb the way I climb a rock wall, grabbing whatever I can find and using all my muscles to pull myself up. I finally settle inside, my feet barely touching the floor. A St. Christopher medallion is clipped to the visor, and a leather string with a wood cross hangs from the rearview mirror. The truck has an extended cab, and in the back seat are a piñata stick and an orange life buoy.

Soon Reynaldo and I are leaving town, driving past the London neighborhood, the point where Weber Street turns into a road with a number instead of a name. The cotton plants are just starting to peep from the ground. I try to count the windmills, but it's impossible. I reach into my backpack and take out the sketch pad and the box of colored pencils. I draw the fields and the windmills, but instead of the streamlined, white design, I draw colorful pinwheels towering over farmhouses and barns.

"So you're an artist!" Reynaldo says.

"I doodle."

"No, no, no. Doodling is what you do with a stick in the dirt or with a pencil in the margins of the city council agendas. But this, my friend, is art. You have taken a scene, and instead of drawing it as is, you have drawn it as you *wish* it were, a landscape full of color and whimsy and delight!"

I smile at the compliment. "I'd rather draw than take pictures."

"Another reason to visit Tres Leches! I can't wait to show you the town. You'll need ten sketchbooks to capture its spirit, and even ten may not be enough."

Inwardly, I cheer. Soon I'll have a new place and new people to draw.

"What's it like in Tres Leches?" I ask.

"Oh, you're going to love it," Reynaldo says. "Along Main Street, there's the Campos Bakery, Panadería Flores, García Bakery, and Señor Lynch's Cupcake Corner. And down Avenue A, *more* bakeries, one from the Martínez family and another from the López family. Then there's the DeLeon Shop of Sweets and Boemker's Bake House. The whole town smells like cake!"

"Which bakery has the best recipe for tres leches cake?"

"It's impossible to know, for each baker adds a little twist, but even if I did have a preference, I could never say. As mayor, I must keep my opinions to myself, or the town will accuse me of playing favorites. It's a challenge of the job. I'm always being blamed for something, even though nothing is ever my fault."

Hmm, I think to myself, *isn't that what all politicians say?*

We reach an intersection in a little town called Driscoll. There's a gas station, two silos, and a bunch of signs. San Diego is straight ahead, Robstown is to the right, and Kingsville is to the left. Nothing says Tres Leches, but we turn left anyway. Soon there are signs for more towns—Bishop, Riviera, and Raymondville, but no Tres Leches. Does Reynaldo know where he's going?

"I know Tres Leches is halfway between Corpus Christi and Mexico," I say, "but where is it on the map, exactly?"

He scratches his head. "You mean the coordinates? The latitude and longitude—or is it longitude and latitude? Hmm . . . I don't know." He gets a twinkle in his eye. "But perhaps we should ask the cartographer next time we see him. Only *he* knows the exact location."

"I've never met a real cartographer before," I say.

"Oh, then you're in for a treat. He's quite skilled. He knows every inch of the whole wide world! He's more accurate than that GPS thingy on your phone, especially in Tres Leches, because—I'm embarrassed to admit—it's mostly a dead zone over there."

We pass a few small towns, and when we reach Riviera, Reynaldo takes a right at a sign that points to Falfurrias.

"We're getting closer," he says.

"So where are the signs? I've seen one for every town except Tres Leches."

"Well, we don't advertise. Not yet, anyway. It's on my mayor's to-do list, but I need to fix a few things before I can bring the tourists. Then there'll be plenty of signs, at ten miles and forty miles and sixty-three miles, regular highway signs but also billboards and neon signs and signs that pop up on your phone. The whole world will know about Tres Leches, and the whole world will want to come, but for now, we have to be happy with our nopal." This is the Spanish word for prickly pear cactus, so I'm confused. He must see it on my face, because he points at the road and explains, "It's shaped like a conejo, and that's where we'll turn."

I search for a rabbit-shaped cactus. One looks like a hand with stubby fingers, and another like a cat arching its back, its tail and ears pointing outward. I see nopales that look like snowmen, jester hats, and clapping seals. Finally, there it is! A rabbit, its ears pointing south. Sure enough, Reynaldo flicks on the blinker and turns.

We're on a dirt road now, so the monster truck stirs up dust. When I glance back, I can barely see the highway. Soon it disappears, which makes me a bit nervous because it's my lifeline to Uncle Clem. Perhaps if I wait, the dust will settle and my view of the road will return, but since these giant tires are stirring up continents of dust, I'll have to wait a long time. Then again, I don't want to go back. I want to meet my mother.

I face forward, where the path is clear. Ranch land, mostly, and every now and then, a windmill, but the old-fashioned kind with wooden scaffolds and broad blades. A water tower has toppled and lies half-buried. Up ahead is a splintered post with cardboard signs nailed on it. Some are too faded to read and others too tattered by wind and rain. But one sign is clear, and it says MUD!

I point at it. "What's *that* about?"

"What? You mean I haven't told you? Perhaps not. I might have failed to mention. You see, many things seem obvious, and the obvious never need explanation. Would you dream of mentioning that honey is sweet? Never, am I right? And for that reason—and that reason only—I might have failed to mention the mud. It's human nature to overlook things that are part of the landscape. The blue sky, the green grass, the brown mud." At this, he shrugs. "Thus, we need the sign as a reminder—not a warning, but a reminder—and the reason it's not a warning is because El Cucuy is impervious to mud. Well, maybe not *one hundred percent* impervious, since he slows down a bit and starts sinking if he stands still for more than two minutes, but *mostly* impervious, and mostly is all you need. Don't fear, my young friend. El Cucuy has crossed the mud expanse many times, and all he needs when he gets to the other side is a good bath."

I wasn't worried, but now I'm starting to wonder. Then I see it—the mud—and he's right. It's not a big deal. Just looks like someone left a sprinkler on too long. Now the tires are churning through brown goop instead of dust. We move along slowly but easily, as Reynaldo promised. Then, little by little, the mud deepens. Eventually, the tires are half-buried, but they manage to move along. Then the bushes get shorter—not because they *are* shorter but because they're mostly covered in mud—and because they're mostly covered, they're also mostly dead, their bare clawlike branches groping for the sky. The mud deepens even more. Soon I see no branches at all, only the impressions of them like elbows and knees trying to poke through.

"Are we almost through the mud?" I ask, trying to hold back my fear.

"Well, it's called the *mud expanse*, so it's quite—how do you say?—*expansive*."

Reynaldo's hands grip the wheel tightly. He keeps shifting gears, pressing and letting up on the gas. He leans forward, squinting with concentration, and every now and then, he mutters, "Good boy, Cucuy. Good, good boy." I'm amazed he knows where he's going because there's no road anymore. "Come on, boy, come on!"

I'm saying it, too. "You can do this, Cucuy!"

The tires are moving, but they can't catch hold. We sink. An inch or a foot? It doesn't matter. If we don't get out of here, we'll get stuck.

"Move!" Reynaldo orders, slapping the dashboard.

The vents on top of the hood snort, filling the air with smoke. Reynaldo steps on the gas, and El Cucuy lurches forward.

"He's moving! He's moving!" I cheer.

Slowly, we gain momentum. Reynaldo uses his entire body to drive—his hands on the steering wheel and gears, his feet on the clutch and gas, his head leaning forward and glancing right and left. I'm leaning forward, too. I can't relax. We're making progress, yes, but I'm worried that we'll sink again, the way you sink in water, the way you *drown* in water. What is mud except thick water?! I clutch my hair. Mud and water are the same!

I can't catch my breath. My pulse races, and my hands and feet shake. My heart tightens as if someone's wringing it like a dishrag.

"Are you okay?" Reynaldo asks.

"Just— Just . . ." I can't say more than this.

He reaches over, opens the glove compartment.

"Look in there. That's where I keep the first aid kit."

I reach inside, dig through gardening gloves, latex gloves, weightlifting gloves, fingerless gloves, a baseball glove, and oven mitts. I hold them up, questioning.

"It's called a *glove* compartment!" he explains.

Finally, I spot the first aid kit. I don't know what I expected to find. It's got Band-Aids, more Band-Aids, a pair of tweezers, and Vicks. Meanwhile, my throat feels like it's being squeezed shut. I drop the box and curl into a ball, making myself as tiny as possible, closing my eyes and cupping my hands over my ears, trying my best to shut out the world, to shut out the mud—that water in disguise!

I try to focus on something different, something dry—my shoes, the radio dial, my purse—but it's no use, not with all that sloshing. If only Uncle Clem were here. He always knows how to help. I tell myself to tough it out, but my body doesn't listen. That's the thing about fear—it's not just in the mind, but in the body, too. I can't breathe. I can't calm my heartbeat. I'm going to have a heart attack if I don't calm down!

I'm too lost in my nightmare to notice that the truck is moving faster and that we're finally on dry land. Reynaldo brakes hard to stop, and then he's shaking me.

"Felice! Felice! We're safe! We're free! I told you El Cucuy is mostly impervious."

I look up. We're in a field. Ahead are trees. Behind, the mud expanse. And he's right. We're free.

I open the door and jump out. I've forgotten how tall the truck is, so I tumble when I land. I might have hurt myself, but that's okay because it means the ground is hard and dry.

Reynaldo jumps down, too, and runs over. "Are you okay?"

I'm not, but I can't speak. All that comes out is wheezing as I try to catch my breath. My chest is still tight, my pulse racing. I close my eyes and repeat the phrase *You are on solid ground, you are on solid ground* because Uncle Clem told me to remind myself that I'm safe when I feel threatened. Slowly, my chest relaxes, and I'm finally able to breathe normally.

"Wha— What happened?" Reynaldo asks.

"I had a panic attack."

"Quite understandable. The mud expanse—"

"You don't understand," I say. "I'm deathly afraid of water. Deathly! I was okay until I realized that mud and water are two versions of the same thing."

"When you say *deathly*, do you mean—"

"Just thinking about water freaks me out! I feel like I'm drowning every time. I do everything I can to avoid it. I take sponge baths. I sprint away after flushing the toilet. My uncle took me to the beach once, and then he had to rush me to the ER because I thought I was dying. I didn't even get wet! The very sight of water nearly gave me a heart attack!"

Reynaldo starts pacing. "No, no, no, no, no!"

"It's who I am," I say. "I've gone to counseling and tried

every coping strategy Uncle Clem has come up with, but at the end of the day, I'm still afraid."

He stoops down so he can be at my level. "But, Felice," he says, "how will you ever meet your mother if she won't leave the very watery banks of the very watery river?"

And he's right. How will I ever meet my mother if I can't overcome my fear?

WHO CARES IF IT TAKES THREE DAYS FOR THE HOUR HAND TO MAKE ITS CIRCLE?

EVENTUALLY, I START TO recover from my panic attack. My breath and heartbeat are steady now, but my legs are still wobbly like when I run up the bleachers at school. My palms are sweaty, too, even though my hands are still cold. But it'll pass. It takes my body a little longer than my brain to figure out that I'm safe.

I nod to Reynaldo, and he and I return to the truck. While El Cucuy rumbles along, I study the landscape. It's flat and dotted, with short mesquites and giant live oaks. Then I spot a sign: TRES LECHES, 1 MILE. We're almost there!

Soon, I see it. From here, Tres Leches looks like a town from a cowboy movie. There's a wide central avenue. A few cars are on it, but also bicycles, skateboards, and a horse. I'm eager to see more, but Reynaldo's pulling over. He stops at the side of the road, the monster truck idling with a low growl like a bobcat.

"Before we go into town," he says, "I need to explain some rules."

I rattle off rules I've heard in my neighborhood. "No jaywalking, trespassing, or throwing candy wrappers in the streets."

"Yes, yes, but in Tres Leches, we have some special rules, too."

"Really? Like what?"

"One," he says, holding up a finger, "if you see a giant owl, hide. Two, you can dance in the streets, in the bakeries, and in our beautiful bluebonnet fields, but never, *ever* dance at El Camarón. That's the name of our dance hall and arcade, but it's a terrible place to dance, a *dangerous* place. Three—and this is the most important rule—when you buy something, pay with money."

"What else would I use?" I ask because it seems so obvious.

He thinks a moment, then says, "Let's just say there are people in Tres Leches who prefer the barter system, and it's never a fair trade. I know a guy who traded a goat for a stick of gum."

"Really? Why? Gum doesn't cost much at all."

"It cost him a goat and a whole lot more if you think about it. At the time, however, he thought it was a very delicious stick of gum."

I can't imagine it. The taste of gum lasts only for a minute.

"Do you understand these rules?" Reynaldo asks. I nod, but he isn't satisfied. "Repeat them so I can make sure."

"One," I say, "hide from giant owls. Two, no dancing at El Camarón. And three, use money to buy things."

"Very good! Very, very good." He pauses as if trying to remember something.

"Did you forget to mention another rule?" I ask.

"Not a rule, exactly, but some advice." He takes a deep breath before continuing. "It's probably best to keep your identity a secret. The townspeople are a bit upset about your mom, since she haunts the river, and they're known to blame children for the actions of their parents."

I nod. "I'll just tell them my name's Felice, and I won't mention my mom until after she's no longer a ghost."

"Perfect! And now, my young friend, you are ready for Tres Leches. Prepare to be amazed." He steps on the gas and gets back on the road, bragging the whole time. "I can't wait to show you the sweetest place in Tejas. The bell peppers, the town square, the cakes, the clock with an hour hand that actually moves, the ..."

He keeps rambling, but I'm too focused on the scenery to hear more. He's absolutely right. Every other shop's a bakery. I roll down the window, and the air smells like sugar. The storefronts have large awnings, and every bakery has a couple of bistro tables where people sip coffee and eat dessert. Along the sidewalks are dozens

50

of chimeneas in all different sizes and each with unique paintings of birds, coyotes, or suns. The street is lined with a mixture of parking spots, bike racks, and hitching posts. Reynaldo swerves along because he's trying to avoid bell peppers, which for some reason are planted all over the street.

Finally, he parks, but before leaving the truck, he reaches in the back for the piñata stick.

"Why are you bringing that piñata stick?" I ask.

"What? This? Do you like it? I made it myself. It used to be a boring broomstick, but I glued on these pink and blue streamers to give it new life."

"So we're going to a party?"

Instead of answering, he jumps out. Then he walks over to my side and offers a hand to steady me as I exit his giant truck.

"The piñata stick?" I say, wanting an explanation.

"It's a symbol of my mayorly self. Think about it." He straightens up, clears his throat, and lifts his piñata stick like he's Lady Liberty. "The judge has his gavel, the knight has his sword, the baker has his rolling pin, and the mayor . . . well . . . the mayor has his piñata stick!"

He takes a bow, and I clap. It's really quite the performance.

"And now, my friend, we need sustenance after our long, perilous journey." He waves his arm to showcase the street. "Choose wisely, for you are about to experience your first slice of"—he pauses, and I imagine a drumroll—"tres leches cake!"

I'm not sure which bakery to choose because there are too many, so I pick the nearest, La Michoacana. We step inside, and everyone says hello to the mayor.

"Go place your order," he whispers, nodding to the people waiting at the counters of pan dulce. "I must greet my constituents."

I get in line, and two men take their place behind me. They're talking loudly, making fun of people, how one guy looks like a frog and another guy looks like "a mangy cat with a chewed-off ear."

Two women are in front of me, and one's saying, "Did you hear about Thelma's son?"

"Yes," says the other. "He ran away just like those other kids, and now all she does is cry, la pobrecita."

"Well, if you ask me, it's her fault. She should have been a better parent. He probably left because he couldn't stand being in that house."

"I'm just glad she won't be in the PTA anymore. She was always voting against us."

I know I shouldn't be eavesdropping, but I can't help it—they're standing right there, and they don't seem to care that I'm listening. They go on about someone's husband who's always gambling and someone else's husband who's always drinking.

Since they seem to know so much about everyone, I

have to ask. "Excuse me," I say, tapping the first lady's shoulder. "What do you know about La Llorona?"

She gasps. Then she leans over to meet me eye to eye, and in a harsh whisper says, "Ella es un monstruo." She squints at me, studying me. *Oh no! What if she recognizes me?*

"I'm sorry," I say. "I'm new here, and I heard—"

"Wailing? Did you go near the river?"

I nod, lying but hoping to learn more about my mother.

"Don't ever go to the river," she tells me. "La Llorona will call for you, and the moment she sees you, she'll grab you and—"

"She'll force you under the water," the second woman says. "She drowns everyone who gets near, just like she drowned her children all those years ago."

"But she couldn't have drowned her children, not on purpose," I say.

"She did," the first woman replies. "Out of spite."

"She wanted to punish their father because he played her for a fool."

"Yes, a fool," the first woman says, turning to her friend, "just like el señor Vásquez, whose wife . . ."

They're on to a new bit of gossip, but I'm not listening anymore. How can they say such terrible things about my mother? There's no way she hurt us on purpose. Is that what people really think?

Tres Leches may be the sweetest place in Tejas, but it sure doesn't have the sweetest people.

Finally, it's my turn to order. The server's wearing a pink dress, a white apron, and a cute paper hat. When she catches me staring at it, she says, "Want one?" Then she grabs something that looks like a napkin. "It's called a soda jerk," she tells me as she unfolds it and presses it onto my head. "Looks good on you."

"Thanks," I say, her gift cheering me up a bit.

"So what would you like?" she asks.

"A slice of tres leches cake, please."

Before she can get me a slice, someone grabs my soda jerk. I turn around. It's Reynaldo.

"Did you pay for this?" he asks, spinning the cap on his piñata stick.

"Hello, Mayor," the server says. "I gave it to her."

He reaches in his pocket. "Well, here's a quarter for it."

She shrugs and puts it in the tip jar. "You don't have to pay when it's a gift," she says.

He ignores her as he hands me the hat. I put it in my backpack, planning to draw on it later.

I reach into my purse to pay for my dessert.

"No need," she says. "The first slice is free."

I glance at Reynaldo, remembering his rule. He's already slapping a dollar on the counter.

"We aren't trading anything," she says. "It's free!"

"We'll pay," he insists.

She shrugs again, takes the dollar, and gives me the slice. I sit at a table and put a piece of cake in my mouth. It's so moist, simultaneously sugary and pineapple tart. I let each spoonful linger on my tongue a moment, relishing the tickling sweetness. I eat as slowly as I can, wanting the taste to last forever. After my final bite, I lift the plate to slurp the puddle of milk that remains, closing my eyes to savor it. How could Uncle Clem keep me from tres leches cake all these years?

"All done?" Reynaldo asks.

I shake my head because there's a crumb left. I press my finger against it and lick it off. Not a molecule of cake remains. *Now* I'm done.

"Well, what do you think?" Reynaldo says. "It's delicious. Am I right or am I right?"

"You are absolutely, positively, undeniably and without question, one hundred percent right!"

"I knew it!" he cheers. "And now, my young friend, it's time for the grand tour of our lovely town."

Reynaldo and I walk down Main Street. Now and then, he skips a few steps. He's as excited as a boy showing off his favorite Lego creation. We spot one of his campaign signs. It's got a picture of his belt buckle. I guess that's his logo. "My first term as mayor is almost up," he says as he straightens the sign. "And I say first term because I'm hoping to get a second and a third." He holds up his piñata stick again. He seems to do this every time he's about to make an announcement. "I, Reynaldo Martínez de la Peña, want to be the best mayor in the entire history of Tres Leches!"

I can't help it. I have to clap, and I sincerely hope that he gets reelected. There are quite a few posters for him, but there are also posters for Bonita, the *o* of her name shaped like a heart. I remember hearing about her when I spied on Reynaldo and Uncle Clem yesterday. No wonder Reynaldo was complaining. She's his political rival.

We walk along, Reynaldo pointing his piñata stick at the town clock. "See that? It works again!"

I glance at my watch. Looks like the town clock is a couple of hours behind—or ahead—it's impossible to know when there's no a.m. or p.m. "They don't match," I say.

Reynaldo shrugs. "Who cares if it takes three days for the hour hand to make its circle? At least it moves. It hadn't moved for a whole decade before I fixed it." He taps the side of a mailbox. "Another victory! The mail gets delivered once a month instead of never at all." Then he sidesteps a pothole filled with dirt for bell peppers. I wanted to ask about them earlier, but now there's no need because he's already explaining. "One of my greatest achievements. Bell peppers grow in *all* the potholes along Main Street because *I* planted them. Instead of having dangerous holes in the ground, we have plants." He stoops to smell one. "Mmm . . . I can almost taste the fajitas, kebabs, and arroz con pollo."

As we walk along, he waves at the townspeople. Some wave back, but others point and whisper. I start to feel self-conscious because they're probably talking about me, wondering who I am. What will they say when they discover that I'm the daughter of La Llorona? One lady openly stares at me. A little boy points, and his father doesn't bother to mention that it's rude.

Reynaldo doesn't notice. He's too happy twirling his piñata stick. Then he tosses it in the air and tries catching it behind his back but misses and gets whopped on the head. He rubs the sore spot. "I'm a piñata." He chuckles. "A piñata filled with the sweet candy of pride."

Once again, he counts his accomplishments—the clock, the mail, the bell peppers. "Plus, I organized a fund-run to keep the Mesquite Bean Inn open for the tourists who will come someday—*any* day—maybe tomorrow. How could they *not* visit when all these bakeries line Main Street?" Reynaldo sniffs the air. "Delicious! The empanadas, the cuernitos, the marranitos, but especially the tres leches cakes—they inspire me! We'll have a bake-off!" he announces. "People will travel from around the world to taste our pan dulce, for this is Tres Leches, Tejas, the sweetest—"

He stops, mid-thought, his mouth agape. I follow his gaze to a giant digital billboard that looms over the town. Even now, we're standing in its shadow. "This . . . can't . . . be," he mutters.

The billboard says REAL-TIME POLLING RESULTS. It shows a bar graph, one bar beneath Reynaldo's name and another beneath Bonita's, and they're shifting slightly, Reynaldo's dropping while Bonita's is rising.

"What's wrong?" I ask. "You're still ahead."

"But am I *clearly* ahead? I have only a three percent lead in the current polls! I don't understand. I've done so much for this town."

"¡Mentiras!" someone sneers.

We turn around. A dozen people stand there, glaring. They've been gathering as we studied the polls, but we were too preoccupied to notice. Now they're saying stuff like "Empty campaign promises!" and "You're full of it!" and "We demand answers!"

Reynaldo tightens his grip on the piñata stick.

"The mud!" a baker shouts. He pounds his fist and sneezes at the puff of flour erupting from his hands. "How many cars have gotten stuck? How many people?"

"And our children . . . they should be studying or doing chores," a lady complains—a teacher, I'm guessing, because she's holding a stack of papers and has a red pencil tucked behind her ear. "Instead they're out all night at the dance hall doing who knows what!"

At that, a teenage boy speaks up, but not in favor of the dance hall. "Those peppers all over the street. We have to swerve our bikes and skateboards to avoid them. My best friend sprained his wrist!"

"And I'm always missing my appointments because of that clock." A viejita points her cane at the clock on City Hall, and everyone looks at it, then down at their watches. They tsk-tsk and shake their heads.

"Amigos. ¡Amigos!" Reynaldo says. He backs up, and we get separated as the people edge forward, blocking my way. For a moment, I can't see him, but then he hops onto a truck bed that looks like it was abandoned a long time ago. It probably got a flat from one of the potholes—the potholes that no longer exist, thanks to his ingenious solution. A squirrel on the hood twitches its tail in a dozen directions, and even *that* seems angry and loud.

"Order! Order!" Reynaldo says, banging his piñata stick. "¡Escúchenme, escúchenme!"

Everyone hushes, responding to his authority. He *is* the mayor, after all.

I'm ready to listen, too, but something else gets my attention—the clashing sound of overturning trash cans and a girl yelling, "Leave him alone!" Then I hear scuffling and someone going, "Aaahhh!"

I know Reynaldo needs me, but it sounds like someone else might need help, too. What do I do? Stay with a new friend or go to a stranger?

"Aaahhh!" I hear again.

For the moment, Reynaldo has things under control, so I head toward the sound of someone in trouble.

I CAN'T BELIEVE THOSE KIDS
LISTENED TO YOU

I FOLLOW THE NOISE and turn into an alley, where I'm hit with the stench of rotten eggs. It overpowers everything, souring the sweet scent of honeysuckle and tres leches cake. I crinkle my nose, wanting to step away but also curious to see what's happening.

There's a boy on the ground. He has a high pompadour, the highest I've ever seen, and the poor guy's scurrying backward as three kids kick dirt at him. There's a girl, too, with lots of feathers in her hair. She's wearing dark goggles and a shirt embroidered with flowers across the yoke. She's behind the kids, trying her best to reach the boy, but they're blocking her path.

"Where's my sister?" one of the bullies asks.

The pompadour boy just shakes his head.

"The last time anybody saw her, she was with your father."

"Then . . . then . . . ask my father," the pompadour boy says.

"Yeah!" the feather girl adds. "You can't blame Rooster for whatever his father does."

"Says the daughter of a witch," the bully answers.

He and the others kick more dirt at the boy. For a minute, I'm stuck processing what I just heard about the girl being related to a witch. Yesterday, this would have frightened me, but not today. After all, I'm related to La Llorona, so I can understand how this girl might feel.

"Hi!" I say in my friendliest voice because I'm remembering Cammy from my walk yesterday and how Uncle Clem always says that biscuits calm the meanest dogs. When the bullies turn around, I see that I'm dealing with two boys and a girl. "I'm Felice. Nice to meet you." I hold out my hand, but they just look at it, confused.

The tall guy lifts his chin at me as if to say, "Hey." Then the other boy lifts his chin. Then the girl. I can tell they're trying to figure out whether I'm in the "friend" or "foe" category.

"Is that a friendship bracelet?" I ask the girl. "Did you make it yourself?"

She nods.

"I love how you combined the green and pink," I say. "It reminds me of a beautiful rose garden."

"Um . . . I never thought of it that way, but . . . I guess?"

I walk to the side of the alley, where three skateboards lean against the wall. "Are these yours?"

"Yeah," the tall guy says. "You skate?"

"No. I can't even jump rope without tripping."

The second guy starts bragging. "I can jump rope and skateboard at the same time. I can play basketball and baseball from a skateboard, too."

"Really? Wow!" I'm being sincere. He must be very talented. "What else can you do?"

"Kick-flips, heel-kicks, grinds, and ollies."

"I really admire people with athletic skills," I say. This, too, is the truth. "Hey, can you hop over all those bell peppers in the street? Because I'd love to see it. If you don't mind, that is."

"Easy-peasy," he says, smiling as he takes off and hops over the first bell pepper in his path. I clap and say, "Way cool!" Then the tall guy follows, choosing a taller bell pepper and adding a spin as he jumps. "That's so impressive!" I call out.

The girl's getting her skateboard, too, but before leaving, she points at the feather girl and the pompadour boy. "Stay away from those two," she warns. "They're monsters."

She takes off, and when she glances back, I give a little wave even though I'm glad to watch those mean kids leave. In my opinion, bullies are the real monsters.

When I turn toward the alley, the boy is standing up, brushing dirt and garbage from his clothes. He's dressed like any regular kid with a T-shirt and jeans, but his shoes—black, patent leather, and pointy-tipped—

are the kind made for tuxedoes. He takes a rag and a tin of polish from his back pocket and starts buffing his shoes right away. They soon shine like glass, and I can't help thinking of Cinderella at the ball, if she were a boy and had black instead of clear slippers.

"Thanks for helping us out," the girl says as she picks up the metal trash cans and replaces the lids.

"Yeah, thanks," the boy echoes. "I can't believe those kids listened to you. You asked them to skate away, and they did. What's your secret? I gotta know your secret. No one ever listens to me. I couldn't convince a fish to swim or a toad to croak if I tried. And believe me, I have tried."

The girl shakes her head. "Quit being so dramatic, Rooster."

I realize now that he's the one who stinks. The rotten egg smell is overwhelming. I hold back my gag reflex, not wanting to hurt his feelings.

"So that's your name?" I ask, trying to distract myself from the smell. "Rooster?"

"Yeah," he says.

I glance at the girl.

"I'm Ava," she reveals.

Then I tell them my name even though they probably remember from when I told the bullies. "I'm sorry those kids were being mean," I say.

"We're used to it," Rooster admits. "Stuff like this happens every day."

I don't ask, but I guess that it's because he stinks like rotten eggs and she wears super-large, super-dark goggles. If it were up to me, things like that wouldn't matter, but they seem to matter to everyone else.

I want to know why that skateboarding girl said they were monsters, but before I have a chance to ask, a squirrel runs into the alley, hops onto a trash can, and starts flicking his tail and doing rapid hand gestures. I give him another look. I think it's the squirrel I saw a few minutes ago, the one on the hood of the abandoned truck.

"Slow down, Paco," Ava says.

The squirrel sighs, then repeats his tail flicks and gestures. I don't understand any of it, but Ava's going "Hmm . . ." and "Really?" and "Tell me more."

When he finishes, Ava interprets, not for me but for Rooster. "The town's complaining again, this time about the river."

"Not our problem," Rooster says.

"Agreed," Ava replies.

It may not be their problem, but it's certainly mine. "Well, nice meeting you," I say before rushing back into the street, where even more people have gathered. They're packed tight, shoulder to shoulder, an angry mob.

A man with a handlebar mustache is standing on a bistro table and shouting at Reynaldo, "You promised to make the river safe again. But it's still dangerous. Children have drowned there."

I gulp. He must be talking about Gustavo and Henry, my brothers. For a minute, I side with the crowd, glad they've not forgotten about the tragedy, but then I notice Reynaldo. He's trembling and is almost as blue as his guayabera because he's holding his breath. And then I remember . . . he knew my brothers. They were his best friend's sobrinos. He wants the river to be safe again, too. That's why he went to Corpus Christi to see Uncle Clem.

There's a moment of silence, but it doesn't last long.

"It's cursed!" someone shouts. "Because of La Llorona, we can't go to the river, *ever*!"

"Amigos," Reynaldo tries, backing up as the crowd approaches the truck. "Order! Order!" he says, his piñata stick like a gavel, but they keep coming.

"We want to go fishing again."

"We want to go tubing."

"And skinny-dipping! Remember when we used to go skinny-dipping during the full moon?"

"When you ran for mayor," the man with a handlebar mustache says, "you promised to fix the clock, the mail, and the potholes, but you *won* because you promised to make the river safe again."

"We need a new mayor!" a woman shouts.

"¡Eso!"

"Now we're talking!"

"Wait, wait, wait, wait!" Reynaldo says.

He keeps looking over our heads. I turn around. It's the billboard. He's quickly losing ground. His 3 percent lead has fallen to 1 percent, and now he and Bonita are even!

He straightens and holds up his piñata stick. *Yes, Reynaldo, yes! Give them a speech.*

"As it says on the poster at the community center," he begins, pausing to build the suspense. The audience listens. "You cannot step into the same river twice!"

His voice is triumphant, but it doesn't last. Once again, a baker pounds his fist. "Well, I'd be happy to step in it once!"

Everyone agrees.

"You said it!"

"We don't care about the clock. We care about the river!"

"Yeah, what happened to reversing La Llorona's curse?"

They keep edging forward.

"Order! Order!" Reynaldo calls again, banging his piñata stick. "¡Escúchenme, escúchenme!"

"Enough!" we hear. It's a commanding voice, and everybody hushes. In fact, the crowd parts to make way for a woman in a lab coat, the hem of a red dress peeking out from beneath. She's escorted by two muscular men wearing green aprons, and when she reaches the truck, the men support her as she jumps onto the make-shift stage. Then they face the crowd, cross their arms, and stare at us.

Meanwhile, the woman nods at Reynaldo and offers her hand in greeting. Her dark hair is pulled into a tight bun. She's drawn thick lines around her eyes, adding a curl toward the temples. With her lipstick, she's traced a heart, using the curves of her upper lip for the top and a perfectly centered point for the bottom. It makes her mouth look very small. That's when I realize . . . this must be Bonita!

"You will never free the river," she tells Reynaldo. Then, to the crowd, she says, "He will never free the river! If you fools had voted for me in the last election, we wouldn't be dealing with this problem anymore."

"It is a big problem, I admit," Reynaldo explains. "But I have some ideas—bridges and dams, professional life-guards, and . . . and . . . life buoys, lifeboats, Life Savers! No, wait, that's a candy."

"Spoken like a true handyman," Bonita says. "I can't believe you people fell for him, a man who thinks he can fix things with his hands."

"I can," Reynaldo says. "The clock, the potholes!"

Bonita ignores him. "Mi gente," she says to the crowd. "Our mayor brags about fixing the clock and the potholes, about driving his truck across the mud to get our mail once a month, and all this is true. But some things"—she points at a new pothole—"are meant to be fixed, while others"—she nods in another direction, probably toward the river—"are meant to be healed. I am a pharmacist, a healer. I can prove my abilities to you, but it will cost."

"Wait, wait, wait!" Reynaldo pleads. "I *will* fix the river. I'll fix it before our debate in two days."

"I'll *heal* it sooner than that," Bonita counters.

"I pledge to all of you," Reynaldo says. "I will fulfill my campaign promise. I was just attending to other matters first."

No one's listening. They're too busy discussing Bonita's proposal, how they'll get to go fishing, swimming, tubing, and skinny-dipping again.

"Order, order!" Reynaldo cries.

Meanwhile, Bonita crosses her arms with a smug smile on her face. I know I shouldn't judge people before spending time with them, but I don't trust her. How does she plan to "heal" the river? Something tells me that her "medicine" won't be good for my mom.

"Reynaldo! Reynaldo!" I call, but he can't hear me over all the noise. "Which way to the river?" I ask the nearest person because I need to get there before Bonita. "Which way to the river?" I ask over and over again, but all I get are arms shooing me away.

I glance back toward the alley. Ava and Rooster must know where it is, but they're slipping into the shadows. I chase after them. "Wait for me!" I yell out. But when I get to the alley, they're gone.

WE'RE JUST MAKING SURE YOU'RE CORPOREAL

LUCKILY, THE SCENT OF sulfur is strong. I sniff the air, turning my head this way and that, trying my best to determine where Rooster and Ava went. The scent leads me through more alleys and down deserted streets, through shadows and dark corners, sometimes to spaces behind fences or beneath cars.

Finally—finally!—I spot them at the edge of town on a dirt road. On Rooster's shoulder is a boom box, and on Ava's is Paco, the squirrel.

"Hey!" I call out.

They turn around. As soon as they spot me, Ava and Paco put their hands on their hips. "Are you following us?" Ava scolds.

"You should go back," Rooster warns.

"Where are you going?" I say, still approaching.

"Of course she doesn't listen to me," Rooster mutters to himself. "No one ever listens to me."

"Can you tell me where the river is?" I ask. "Once you tell me, I'll be on my way."

Ava and Rooster glance at each other, but instead of giving me directions, Ava says, "The river's off-limits."

"I know, but I have to go there."

"Why?" Now she and Paco cross their arms as if daring me to answer.

Should I tell them? Can I trust them? What will they do if they find out I'm the daughter of La Llorona?

I decide not to take a chance. "I helped you earlier, remember? Can't you do me a favor in return?"

Ava thinks a moment but shakes her head. "It's like this: Even with directions, you'll probably get lost, but even if you don't get lost, you'll probably fall in the river and—"

"I know," I say, cutting her off because the next word is *drown* and I'll panic if I hear it again. Just thinking about it is making my hands go cold.

"You should go back to town," Rooster says, "where it's safe."

He and Ava turn around and start walking again, but no way am I ready to give up. I run in front of them to block their path.

"Look," I say. "I'm new here. I don't know my way around. Mayor Reynaldo was going to take me to the river, but he has his hands full right now. And I really need to go! It's the whole reason I'm here."

"Maybe she doesn't know," Rooster says to Ava. And then to me, "The river's cursed. That's why it's off-limits. We're just trying to protect you."

Ava nods. "We're trying to protect ourselves, too," she adds. "We already get blamed for people who go missing. No need to add *you* to the list."

She must be referring to the runaway I heard about at the panadería and to the bully's missing sister. I start thinking about what the skateboarding girl told me earlier.

"Missing people? Is that why they call you monsters?"

Ava stomps her foot. "Who said that? Because it's not true!"

"That's right," Rooster joins in. "We are not monsters. We try to help people do the right thing, but no one listens."

"But your father," I say to him, then turning to Ava, "and your mom. Those kids earlier were talking about them."

"Everybody around here talks about everybody else," Ava replies. "Besides, can we help it if we're related to people who cause trouble sometimes?"

I take a moment before replying. Maybe I should tell them the reason I want to go to the river. Maybe if they know that I'm also related to someone who gets blamed for trouble, they'll help because they'll see that I'm just like them.

"I understand," I say, "because ... well ... because my mom is ... she's ... okay ... she's ..." I didn't realize it would be so hard to admit the truth. At this rate, it'll take three hours to finish speaking, so I close my eyes and spit it out. "My mother is La Llorona."

They squint at me, probably trying to decide whether to believe me. Then Rooster approaches and lightly pokes my left shoulder while Ava pokes my right one. Then he pokes and she pokes, back and forth, three or four more times.

I step back and rub my arms. "What are you guys doing?"

"You felt that?" Ava asks.

"Of course I felt it. How could I not?"

"We're just making sure you're corporeal," she explains.

"I *am*. Skin and bones, see? I cast a shadow. Look!" I point at the ground.

"It's a very distinct shadow," Rooster admits.

"Just because my mom's a ghost doesn't mean that I am, too."

"And just because my father's a devil doesn't mean that I'm a devil," Rooster adds.

"And just because my mom's an owl-witch . . ." Ava begins, touching one of the feathers in her hair and then shrugging.

"Reynaldo found me," I explain, "so I can meet my mother. She thinks I drowned that day, but I didn't. Once she knows that I'm okay, she'll stop crying. She'll stop haunting the river. It'll be safe again, and my mother and I will finally be together."

Ava and Rooster look at each other, a dozen expressions crossing their faces. First, they seem to be asking each other a question. Then they shake their heads and nod, and then shake them again as if saying "no, yes, no." Finally, they shrug, which probably means "maybe." And after all this, Paco joins in, miming. He opens his mouth and closes his eyes as if crying. He lifts his arms like a scary ghost and embraces himself. Then he flaps his arms like he's got angel wings. I have no idea what he's saying.

"Paco's right," Rooster concludes. "We have to help her."

Ava teases him. "You're such a softie." Then, to me, "Listen, we want to help, but you're talking about going to a cursed river. We already have enough curses. And why should we do something that helps the town? It has a few nice people, like Mayor Reynaldo, but most don't want us around. All they see are the children of monstruos."

"Then make them see something else," I tell her.

"Imagine what the people will think if you help make the river safe again. You'll be heroes!"

"I don't need to be a hero," Rooster says, "but it sure would be nice to be accepted."

He and Ava look at each other. I can tell they're silently communicating again, making a decision, hopefully in my favor. I'm still standing on the path in front of them, and they walk right past me. When I turn around, all I see are their backs as they walk away, and I hang my head because I failed. I thought I had made a convincing argument, but apparently they want nothing to do with me.

I don't know their stories, but the tragedy of my mother's story weighs me down. I hate knowing that she's been calling for me all these years, and worse, that we've missed all this time together and that she's been alone. How can people complain about her? How can they call her a monster when all she wants is her children? Can't they see the bigger problem here? My mom was abandoned twice, first by my dad and then by the town, and now I'm being abandoned by Rooster and Ava. Sure, they don't owe me anything, but can't they find it in their hearts to help? Sometimes when I'm angry, I cry, but other times, I clench my fists, wishing for something to punch, like now because I'm starting to understand why Uncle Clem wanted to leave this place. He wanted to shield me from all these mean people.

Fine, then. I'll head back to town and look for someone else to show me the river. Maybe Reynaldo has found a way to escape the crowd, and we can return to our original plan.

"Hey, Felice!" Ava calls. "What are you waiting for? This is the way to the river."

"You're going to take me there?" I ask, surprised.

"If that's what you still want."

I can't believe it! They're actually going to help after all. "It is!" I call back, running to catch up to them. "Thanks!"

"Don't thank us yet," Rooster says. "You might not like what you find."

I ignore him. He doesn't know what he's talking about. My mother's at the river. I'm going to *love* what I find.

THE BLUEBONNET IS OUR STATE FLOWER

WE WALK IN SILENCE, probably because we're not exactly friends yet, so I'm not sure what to talk about. Every now and then, Ava stops to examine a plant and Rooster shifts his boom box from one shoulder to the other.

Little by little, the grass overtakes the road, and soon we're on a narrow path that very quickly disappears because suddenly we're in a field with thousands of bluebonnets. I've seen them along highways or in vacant lots around the city, but I've never seen so many in one place before. When a breeze runs through, the shimmering flowers look like a rippling lake. I squint, trying to fool myself into thinking I'm standing, unafraid, at the edge of the sea, and then I realize that this *is* a type of sea, one that's made of blooms.

We take a few steps into the field, but we don't go far before Ava kneels to inspect the flowers at our feet. I don't question it at first because she seems to love plants. "The bluebonnet is our state flower," she mumbles to herself. "I think I'll pick a few and add them to my garden."

Paco sprints across the field, and when he reaches the far side of it, he frantically twitches his tail. He seems alarmed. I still don't understand the sign language of squirrels, but I can tell he wants us to hurry. I want us to hurry, too. My mother's calling for me, and I've waited my whole life to meet her. Then again . . .

"I shouldn't let this beauty go to waste," I say, mostly to myself because really I'm just thinking aloud. I sit, reach into my backpack, and take out my sketchbook and pencils. I draw—first the field, then a single bluebonnet, and then another that's slightly different. In fact, no two flowers are the same. The only way to remember them all is to capture each in a drawing.

"The bluebonnet is our state flower," Ava mumbles again. "And there are six types of bluebonnets, some that aren't even blue."

The whole time, Rooster's saying, "We need to keep going. Get up. Get up! You can't stay here forever. Come on. Let's move. This field is enchanted. You'll be stuck for another month if you don't move."

Ava and I wave him off. Why's he making so much noise? He should stop worrying and smell the roses. Or should I say *the bluebonnets*? Yes, the bluebonnets. Look at how beautiful they are. They aren't actually blue, now that I think about it. They're a little purple, but not exactly purple, either. The color lies somewhere between blue and purple, a sort of blue violet. I look back at the sketches I've already drawn. They're all wrong. I need to redo them. I must capture the color exactly.

"Felice?"

"Yes, Rooster, what do you want? Move aside. Your shadow's blocking the light."

"May I have this dance?"

"Sure. Of course. Let me gather my things."

I put away my pencils and sketch pad, loop the straps of my backpack around my shoulders, and readjust my happy face emoji purse. Rooster's already in a formal dancing pose, waiting, so I grab his hand and shoulder. That's when I hear it—music—and there's Paco in the middle of the field, holding up the boom box.

"It's the 'Blue Danube,'" Rooster says. "I thought it'd be a good choice since we're in a field of *blue*bonnets."

He starts to lead—a slow one-two-three, one-two-three—as we waltz across the field. Our steps, their rise and fall, are like gentle waves, and once again I pretend that I'm on the sea, having conquered my fear of water. How I wish it were true, but as we continue to dance, reality sets in. I'm not dancing on a lake, but in a field. I'm here because I'm looking for my mother who lives by a river. I must approach this river even though I'm deathly afraid of water. I repeat to myself, *I'm dancing in*

a field, waltzing with Rooster, going to a river to meet my mom.

Soon we've crossed the bluebonnets, and the "Blue Danube" clicks to a stop.

I blink my eyes a few times and give my head a little shake. "What . . . what happened?" I ask. "Where's Ava?"

"She's still stuck," Rooster answers, pointing.

I search. From this distance, she looks tiny. I don't think she realizes we've left.

"The flowers are enchanted," he says. "I kept trying to get you both to leave, but all Ava wanted was to pick flowers, and all you wanted was to draw."

I reach into my backpack. Looks like there are a dozen new sketches. "How long have we been here?"

"About an hour," Rooster says. "Now if you'll excuse me, I have to help Ava."

He races across the field and nods to Paco, who pushes the replay button for the "Blue Danube," and before I know it, he and Ava are dancing. She looks like a zombie—not because she's gory, but because she's moving without purpose, just mindlessly following Rooster's lead. Is that how I looked a few minutes ago? Then Rooster adds a few more steps, turning her and spinning her beneath his arm. Ava laughs, and the closer they get, the more aware she seems. By the time they reach me, she's chattering away.

". . . and I couldn't stop listing bluebonnets facts. I

think I was repeating them. I kept saying, *The blue-bonnet is our state flower*, like I was reciting the Pledge of Allegiance over and over again. I can't believe that I forgot about the bluebonnet field, but it's only here in the spring. The rest of the year, this place is empty. Thank goodness you were with us, Rooster, and that you were smart enough to remember that no one can resist your invitation to dance." She looks at me. "For some reason, the bluebonnets don't affect him."

"Resisting temptation is my special advantage," Rooster admits. "That, and dancing."

Paco returns, lugging the boom box, which he releases the moment he reaches us. The poor squirrel looks exhausted.

"I'm so sorry, little guy," Rooster says, lifting the boom box and planting it on his shoulder once again. "You should have left it in the field. I would have grabbed it myself."

Ava picks up Paco, cradling him and promising extra pecans for all his help.

Paco closes his eyes and smiles. Yesterday, I wouldn't have believed squirrels could smile, but I'm quickly learning that in Tres Leches, all kinds of things are possible.

"So where's the river?" I ask.

"On the other side of these trees," Ava says.

I try to see through them. The path is full of dense

shadows. I can only guess what creatures lurk there, but I'm not discouraged. Spots of sunlight poke through, and I know they lead to my mother.

Rooster and Ava don't waste time. They head into the forest. I take a few steps, too, but then I hold back, afraid, because beyond those shadows is ... is ... water! I could probably face a shallow pond, but we're heading toward a river with a strong current. I've seen videos of fast-moving rivers taking whole houses, their walls and roofs snapping and splintering apart. I grab my fore-arm, feeling for the bones and wondering if they would snap and splinter, too.

"Felice?" It's Ava. She and Rooster have turned around, probably wondering why I'm frozen. "Aren't you coming?"

"I want to," I say, "but I can't seem to move."

"Another spell?" Rooster asks, alarmed.

"No, nothing like that."

"Then what?"

I don't answer right away. This isn't the first time I've been in this situation. My school friends were always inviting me to the aquarium or the beach, and I always said no. First I came up with excuses, but then I decided to tell them about my aquaphobia, how I almost drowned as a baby. "But you won't be in the water at the aquarium," they said, and "There are lifeguards at the beach." But even knowing this, I could never feel safe, so I skipped all those water-related get-togethers. I tried to explain that my fear isn't just in my head, that I have a very physical response with my legs and arms and heart doing their own thing, no matter how hard I try to use logic to convince myself that I'm not in danger. My friends just looked at me, confused. They never said I was weird, but I'm sure they *thought* it.

"What's wrong?" Rooster asks again.

I look at him and Ava, deciding whether to trust them, but I've no choice. They'll be leading me to the river, and there's no way I can fake being brave.

"Well," I try, "I'm . . . how do I say this? . . . I'm terribly afraid of . . . of . . ." It's hard to get the words out, so I whisper, "Of water."

They're quiet for a moment, considering.

"Okay," Rooster says as if it's no big deal.

"You don't think I'm weird?"

"No. Everyone's afraid of *something*."

"It's true," Ava says. "Everyone's afraid of something and *brave* about something else. But if you want, we can look for a curandero."

"A healer?" I ask.

"For los sustos," she explains.

I know *susto* is the Spanish word for shock or fright, but I didn't know a healer could cure me. I've already tried a scientific solution, counseling, and desensitization therapy. In theory, if I'm exposed to a little bit of water each day and then a little bit more and a little bit more, I'll get used to it. That's what *desensitization* means, but so far, it hasn't worked.

The mention of a healer reminds me of Bonita and her promise to "heal" the river right away if the town meets her price. I glance at the sky, trying to figure out the time.

"I can't go looking for a curandero," I say. "I need to get to the river right now, before it's too late."

"It's up to you," Ava says, rushing ahead, but Rooster hangs back, standing beside me and making me feel a little more secure, enough to at least step forward. As we move toward my greatest fear, I try a relaxation technique, something Uncle Clem taught me—breathe in for three counts, breathe out for three counts. I put one foot in front of the other, proud that I'm heading toward water. Little by little, we move along. We're silent, but the twigs beneath our feet are loud. Soon, the spots of sunlight disappear, and in the deeper darkness, we stumble.

"Are you sure you know where we're going?" I ask because I can't see a path anymore.

"Just a moment," Ava says. She pulls down her goggles, letting them hang around her neck. I glimpse her eyes for the first time. They're perfectly round and huge, and in the darkness, they're dilated like a cat's—no—like an owl's! "Much better," she says, scanning the forest. "This way."

We follow as she skillfully leads us around rocks, spiderwebs, fallen logs, and ant piles.

"Ava has superior night vision," Rooster explains. "It's her special advantage."

"She has a special advantage, too?" I ask, remembering what he said about his ability to dance and resist enchanted flowers.

"Yes. Everyone does."

I wonder if it's true, and if so, then what's *my* special advantage? Maybe drawing. I might not be the best, but I'm pretty good. One thing is for sure, though. I don't have an advantage right now. Even though I'm managing to hold back my fear of water, another fear is creeping up because the closer we get to the river, the closer we get to my mom. I shouldn't be afraid of her, but I am—not because she's a ghost but because twelve years have passed. I couldn't even walk the last time she saw me. What if I tell her who I am, and she doesn't believe me? For all she knows, I could be any girl. I could be lying, playing some mean trick on her. Or—and this is even scarier—what if she believes I'm her daughter but doesn't *like* me? What if she's disappointed because I'm such a scaredy-cat around water? Or worse, what if she's mad at me for taking so long to come back? I would have come years ago if I'd known she was here. That's what I want to explain, but what if she doesn't give me the chance?

We walk on, and soon the trees thin out. More and more spots of sunlight return.

"We're almost there," Ava says.

Then she fits the goggles over her eyes again. "I can see in the dark just fine, but seeing in the light is a different story." She does a few adjustments and asks if I'm ready to keep going.

I'm not, but I nod anyway. We take a few more steps and enter a clearing.

"What is this place?" I ask.

"La Llorona Park," Ava says, using air-quotes when saying the last word.

LOOKS LIKE A POSSUM BONE

AT THE FAR EDGE of the clearing, a large square of plywood is nailed to a wooden post. Vines are starting to creep up it, but they haven't reached the sign yet. From this distance, I can't read it, so I step forward, curious to see what it says.

Rooster blocks my path. "Just ignore that old sign. Let's head this way to the river."

I brush him aside, even more curious now.

"Wait! Stop!" Rooster says.

"She should read it," Ava tells him. "She should know what she's dealing with."

As I approach, burrs latch on to my socks, scratching my ankles. A few flies and mosquitoes buzz around. The wood on the sign has become gray and splintered. The words have faded from the sun, but as I get near, I can read them.

BEWARE THE RIVER,
FOR HERE HAUNTS LA LLORONA.
IN LIFE, SHE WAS A FOOL FOR LOVE.

THEN SHE DROWNED HER CHILDREN OUT OF SPITE, AND NOW HER GHOST WANTS TO DROWN YOU, TOO.

I sigh heavily. It's the same story I heard in town.

Ava and Rooster are soon behind me, and Ava puts a hand on my shoulder. "Sorry you had to learn about your mother this way."

I shake my head and rush to defend my mother. "She had a relationship with my father, not knowing he had a wife and family across the river, but I will never believe she drowned her children to get revenge."

"People do terrible things when they're angry," Ava says.

I know this is true. The news is full of stories about people who do terrible things out of anger, even parents who hurt their children. They say love is blind, and maybe my love *is* blind because I refuse to believe that my mom could be so cruel.

"Beyond this sign," Rooster says, "you'll hear her cries. You won't be able to resist her call, and once she sees you, she'll try to drown you."

I shake my head, still refusing to believe.

"Are you sure you still want to go?" he asks.

"She won't hurt me," I say. "I'm her daughter. She'll see that I'm okay, and she'll stop haunting the river. I have to meet her. I've wanted to meet her my whole life."

Rooster and Ava glance at each other. They're like a

brother and sister, knowing each other's thoughts without saying a word.

"We'll be right by your side," Ava says, but Paco has another idea. He crosses his arms and shakes his head no. Ava pats his head. "All right, then, buddy. You stay here where it's safe."

Ava, Rooster, and I move along, and I'm amazed by how strong I feel. I should be hyperventilating by now. My stomach should be twisting and turning like towels in a dryer. I've never been this close to water without panicking. I can only guess it's because I'm more excited about meeting my mom. Could it be? Have I found a cure to my phobia? Replacing my fear with another, stronger emotion?

Suddenly, Rooster stops, making Ava and me stop, too.

"That's strange," he says. "I don't hear La Llorona yet."

Ava turns and tilts her head. "I can't even hear the river."

I close my eyes. Turn and tilt my head just like Ava did a few moments ago. There's a slight rustling in the trees but nothing else.

"Maybe the river's extra slow today," Rooster says. "And maybe La Llorona's extra quiet."

"Maybe," Ava repeats, but she doesn't sound convinced.

There's only one way to find out, so we move forward.

Soon, we reach a cut in the earth, a giant arroyo with tree roots poking out of the sides. We hold on to them as we go down. The bottom of the ditch is rocky, with no plants at all. It's as if a giant came and plucked out all the grasses, all the weeds, and all the trees, uprooting everything. Rooster stoops and picks up a white stick.

"Looks like a possum bone," he says, tossing it and picking up another. "This one's from a rabbit." Then another and another. "Raccoon, skunk, and"—he glances at Ava—"squirrel."

In fact, the ground is littered with the bones of small animals.

"They hear your mother cry," Ava explains, "and they come to her and jump into the river and . . ." She doesn't finish, leaving me to guess what happens next.

"So we're here?" I say. "We're at the river?"

"We're where it used to be," she answers. "This is where it flowed."

I didn't suddenly get courageous, I realize. I didn't panic because there was nothing to panic about.

We walk along, careful not to sprain our ankles on the rocks. But the riverbed is completely dry, not a trickle anywhere. When we spot a trio of large rocks, we sit. It's been a long hike. Now we're here, but the river's gone. It's silent, but maybe . . . maybe . . .

I stand up. "Mom!" I call. "Mom! It's me, Felice. I'm your daughter, remember? I'm here to meet you. I've waited my whole life to meet you!" I listen and wait for a response, cupping an ear in case she's far away.

"Mom!" I try again. "Mom!"

Still nothing.

I take a deep breath, and with every fiber of my being, I scream out for her. "Mooommm!"

My cry echoes, but then it disappears and the whole place goes silent again. Exhausted, I sit back down. Ava and Rooster give me sad smiles.

"We're too late," I say. "Bonita found a way to cure the river. This whole trip has been for nothing."

"She didn't cure the river," Rooster says. "She got rid of it. No river, no Llorona."

He stands, grabs a handful of rocks, and throws them, one at a time. They thud as they hit the ground, but they should be splashing instead. I imagine it—rocks splashing in the water. And that's when I realize . . .

"I know what we have to do," I say. Rooster and Ava give me puzzled looks even though the answer is obvious. "We have to bring the river back! That's the only way I'll get to meet my mom!"

SPRUCE GOOSE SOUNDS A LOT BETTER THAN BIRCH GOOSE

AFTER I ANNOUNCE THAT we need to bring the river back, Rooster and Ava stare at me, waiting for an explanation.

"We need rain," I tell them. "The water will flow to the arroyo, and we'll have a river again."

"My mother made it rain once," Ava says, "but instead of a river, we got mud."

"Are you talking about the mud expanse?"

"Yeah, that's what they call it."

I'm about to ask how her mother made it rain when Rooster does a little tap and hop, the beginning of a dance, but then he stops himself. "I tried rain dancing once, but nothing happened. All I got from it was dirty shoes. Then again, I couldn't make thunder roar or lightning ... light."

His story reminds me of a friend's science project in school, something about how, when a lot of people rain dance, they kick dust particles up to the sky, and in theory those particles are supposed to help it rain.

After realizing this, scientists invented cloud seeding, which has nothing to do with gardening in the sky. It's really about delivering particles, like salt, to the clouds to make it rain.

"I know what we have to do," I say. "If we want to make it rain, we have to deliver a bunch of salt to the clouds."

"You mean by *flying*?" Ava's voice is excited.

"Yes!" I say, excited, too.

Rooster moans. "Here we go again. You're always looking for an excuse to fly, Ava, but you never get off the ground."

"Stop being so negative," she says. "Now that I have a mission, I'm sure to fly."

"So you'll help me?" I ask.

"Absolutely!" Ava says. This is the first time she hasn't hesitated to help.

We turn to Rooster. "I'll help you"—he sighs—"stay out of trouble, that is."

Now that we have a plan, we head back to town to buy salt, picking up Paco along the way and dancing through the bluebonnets again. Meanwhile, Ava goes on and on about flight by telling us the stories of Amelia Earhart, Harriet Quimby, and Bessie Coleman. "I know they all died from plane crashes," she says, "but they're still my heroes. They were women, they were pioneers, and they were brave." And then she goes on about famous airplanes—the Wright Flyer, the *Spirit of*

St. Louis, the Spruce Goose, "which is really made of birchwood, not spruce, but … you know … *spruce goose* sounds a lot better than *birch goose*." She moves on to dirigibles and how they're different from hot-air balloons. She's a walking encyclopedia when it comes to flying. The only reason she stops is because we reach Main Street and—

The bakeries have closed! We go to the nearest one, the DeLeon Shop of Sweets. Its lights are turned off, the glass cases are empty, and the chairs are stacked on tables. The next bakery is also closed, and so is the one two doors down. Across the street, a baker is nailing plywood over the windows and, in red paint, it says, OUT OF BUSINESS. There are other businesses—a florist, a shoe store, and a taco truck—but even though they're open, they've closed their blinds and dimmed their lights. The people walking along the avenue aren't smiling. A few peek into the windows of the empty bakeries. Others sit on benches, bored. A dog pees on one of the bell pepper plants. The only excitement comes from people posting campaign signs for Bonita. The women have copied her style of makeup by painting little hearts on their own lips.

I glance at the billboard. She's now three percentage points ahead of Reynaldo!

I spot a lady walking by. "Excuse me, ma'am?"

She gets a whiff of Rooster and holds her nose. "Speak quickly," she tells me. "It stinks here."

"Why are the bakeries closed?" I ask.

"Haven't you heard?" Her voice sounds funny since she's still pinching her nose. "Bonita got rid of La Llorona—something the mayor never managed to do—and all it cost were the bakers' recipes for tres leches cake."

"But she dried out the river," Ava says. "I thought the whole point was to go tubing and skinny-dipping."

"No," the lady snaps back. "The whole point was to make Tres Leches safe again. No river, no Llorona, no danger."

With that, she walks off, keeping her nose pinched.

I shake my head, stunned. "I can't believe the bakers gave up their recipes, and even though the people got what they wanted, they seem kinda sad."

"You'd be amazed," Rooster says. "People give up all kinds of things when they're upset or scared."

He's right. After all, I gave up fun times with my friends in order to avoid water, and Uncle Clem gave up his hometown because he wanted to protect me from sadness. And just like the people of Tres Leches, we felt safe, but being safe isn't the same as being happy.

"Now we have a new problem," Rooster says, "because we need Bonita in order to get the salt. She won't like knowing what it's for, so if she asks, we'll say we're making jerky."

"Wait a minute!" Ava says. "I'm a vegetarian, remember? She'll never believe we're making jerky." She scratches her head, thinking. "But she might believe we got a giant aquarium and we're prepping it for saltwater fish." Rooster and I nod at this idea. "And you, Felice, are my prima," Ava adds. "We can't tell her you're the daughter of La Llorona, not after she dried up the river and drove your mother away."

Ever since I got here, I've been hiding my identity except from Rooster, Paco, and Ava, but this is the first time I can pretend I have a prima.

I give her a thumbs-up, and we all head to the pharmacy. We step through the doors, and at the registers are the men in green aprons who escorted Bonita a few hours before. They're even more muscular up close. They look like they're in the military with their buzzed haircuts and stern expressions. They don't even smile when they greet the customers or say "thank you for your business" when handing them receipts.

I look away from them to get the layout of Bonita's Pharmacy. It's like Walgreen's, with medicines for colds, allergies, and headaches, but also *unlike* Walgreen's because it has aisles for mal de ojo, susto, and empacho, conditions that are often cured by curanderos. The rest of the aisles are for grocery and cosmetic items, and in the back is an old-fashioned soda fountain where grilled cheese sandwiches, ice cream floats, and tres leches cakes are being sold. This must be the only place that still serves the cake.

Then I see a large display case with a placard that says CURIOS. I walk toward it and study the stuff inside—a pair of glasses, a photo of a goat, a corkscrew, a fiddle, a wedding veil, a castanet, and a whole bunch of other things, including a folder that's labeled RECIPES.

"That's Bonita's collection," Ava says. "Every time she makes a trade, she puts the new item in it." She beckons me away. "Come on. The salt's over here."

Rooster grabs a grocery cart, and he and Ava lead me toward the spices. I don't know how much we need, so we grab every single bag of salt from the shelves.

"Well, well, I thought I smelled trouble," we hear.

We turn to the voice. It's Bonita. She's let down her hair. It's long and lush, and her eyes are dark and warm. Her brows are perfectly plucked and her lashes perfectly curled. Her skin is youthful even though her voice sounds old. She's unfastened a few buttons on her lab coat to reveal more of the silky red dress beneath. She smells like jasmine. I can't help leaning toward her and saying, "You smell nice."

She takes a quick sniff. "I wish I could say the same for . . . all of you." Then she glances at my purse. "How interesting. A purse with heart eyes." Before I can respond, she turns her attention to Rooster. "Muchacho, aren't you tired of stinking? I have the perfect deodorant for your condition." She pulls it out of her coat pocket. It looks like a regular stick of deodorant, but in big letters, it says NEUTRALIZES SCENT OF SULFUR. "And it doesn't cost anything," she says, "if you're willing to trade your shoes for it."

Rooster looks at the deodorant, then at his shoes, then at the deodorant again. I can tell he's tempted. "That's okay," he finally says. "I'll keep my shoes." Reynaldo must have talked to him, told him to always pay with money.

Bonita shrugs, puts the deodorant away. "Suit yourself," she says, glancing at our cart. "My, my. That's a lot of salt."

"We're setting up a saltwater aquarium," Ava quickly explains. "My prima's visiting from out of town, and she loves fish."

"I'm from Corpus Christi," I say, thinking it's a good reason for liking fish, since it's by the ocean. Then again, I never go near the ocean and I don't have feelings for fish one way or another. Maybe they love water, but it's not their fault they have to live in it.

Bonita looks at me, her eyes narrowing. "Setting up an aquarium, huh?"

I gulp, worried she can read my mind. "Um . . . yes?" When she raises one of her thin eyebrows, I repeat myself, this time with more confidence. "Yes, an aquarium. We're going to get a clownfish, like Nemo from that movie."

"That's right," Ava says. "So how much for all this salt and the cart to carry it?"

Bonita considers. "Well, how much do you have?"

Ava and Rooster admit they're broke, so I reach into my purse. "All I have is eighteen dollars."

"That's a shame," Bonita says, "because the total cost is *twenty-five* dollars."

My shoulders droop. I really need this salt. How else can I make it rain?

"However," Bonita adds, "I'll let you have the salt and the shopping cart if you let me have . . . oh, I don't know . . . how about your purse?"

I hold my purse tight against me. Even without Reynaldo's warning, I would never give away my happy face emoji purse. I wish I had enough to pay Bonita. Then again, this isn't the first time I've been without money. I remember losing a ten-dollar bill once and getting all upset and Uncle Clem saying that losing money isn't the end of the world because I could always work to earn more.

"Did you say twenty-five dollars?" I ask Bonita.

"Yes. I'm so sorry it's more than you have."

"That's okay. Hold the salt for us, will you? We'll be right back. Come on, Rooster. Come on"—I wink at Ava—"prima."

When we step outside, I don't give them a chance to ask questions. I head straight to the town square.

There's a lot of hammering going on when we get there. One whole side of the square is filled with wood, ladders, and workers in orange hard hats.

"What are they building?" I ask.

"A stage for the mayoral debate," Rooster says. "It's in two days."

Two days? I have to hurry! Not only for Reynaldo, but for my mother. I'm sure the town's happy that my mother's gone, but they'd be even happier if they had the river, a *safe* river, and if my mother were no longer La Llorona, but a friend, Alegra.

I spot a picnic table, the perfect place to set up. When I get there, I reach into my backpack and take out a large sheet of paper, folding it in half to make a tent for a sign: PORTRAITS FOR $1. Then I take out my sketch pad and pencils.

"What are you up to?" Rooster asks.

"Remember when you told me that your special advantage was dancing and that Ava's was seeing in the dark?"

He nods.

"Well, *my* special advantage is drawing. I don't have enough money to buy the salt, but I can earn it by selling my sketches."

"That's a great idea," Ava says, "but—"

Before she can finish her thought, a banana peel hits her in the back. A group of teens is laughing. One of them has a half-eaten peach and hurls it toward us. It hits the ground near our feet.

Ava sighs, frustrated. "As long as we're here," she explains, "no one will approach you. They hate us around here."

A girl shouts at her, "Your mother must be the only witch that doesn't need a broom to fly!"

I stand up, ready to defend my friend, but Ava stops me.

"Draw your portraits," she says. "Paco can find us when you've earned enough money."

With that, she and Rooster slink away, and the whole time, the teens shout after them: "What happens when you take off your goggles? Do we turn to stone?" and "Chickens lay eggs, but roosters lay *rotten* eggs!" and "Go take another bath in your sulfur pit!"

They laugh and laugh until Rooster and Ava disappear into the shadows.

Someday this town will love them. I'm going to do everything in my power to help people see that Rooster and Ava are nice and talented, no matter how they smell or how they look or who their parents are. I wish I could help them right this minute, but I need to help my mother and Reynaldo first.

I take a deep breath, and like a carnival vendor, I call out, "Portraits! Portraits! Portraits for a dollar!"

People walk by and ignore me. Some even turn in a different direction. When someone glances at me, I say,

"Would you like me to draw your portrait?" They tell me that they'll think about it or come back later. Some don't say anything at all. They just speed away. Paco shakes his head as if disappointed by his community.

I start to feel anxious because no customers means no money, and no money means no salt, and no salt means no rain, and no rain means no river, which means no Llorona, which means I'll never get to meet my mom.

"Anybody want a portrait?!" I shout out, but no one takes me up on my offer.

How will I ever get people to buy portraits? I think this at first, and then I say it out loud, to Paco. He scratches his head a moment. Then he starts to mime, holding an invisible pencil and drawing on invisible paper.

"You want me to draw?" I guess.

He nods.

"But no one's asking for a portrait."

He shrugs as if to say "So what?"

Okay, I'll try his suggestion. It can't hurt. Besides, I like drawing. If anything, it'll help me relax.

I decide to draw people from school, starting with the librarian. I don't draw her in the library, though. Instead, she's pitching books from the baseball field because she's always asking what our interests are, and when we say "robots," she gives us a book on robots *and* a book on artificial intelligence *and* a sci-fi novel. Pitch-ers might throw curveballs, but our librarian throws curve *books*. I also draw the band director blowing into a tuba, and because sounds are invisible, I draw what the notes remind me of. That's why pigs, toads, and baboons are hopping out of the tuba bell. Then I draw my math teacher, Mr. Smith. He's sitting in his wheelchair. I hide numbers all over his portrait—threes for his ears, a six for his nose, fives for the buttons on his shirt, and eights for his shoelaces.

I place the sketches on the picnic table, and Paco finds rocks to weigh them down. Soon, I have a nice display of my work.

"Whatcha doing?" a little girl asks, startling me because I hadn't seen her approach.

"Just drawing."

"Draw *me!*" she says.

I notice a butterfly on her T-shirt, so I draw her sitting on a giant butterfly, her long hair flowing as the two of them soar above the flowers.

"That's me! That's me!" she cheers, grabbing the sketch and running to an old couple sitting on a nearby bench. After she shows them the drawing, they make their way toward me, moving slowly because the man is walking with a cane. He's wearing a fedora, and the woman, a rebozo.

"Can you draw us together?" the viejita asks.

"Of course," I say.

They sit down, and when I notice the woman's locket, I ask her about it.

"Oh, these are my oldest grandchildren," she says, opening it to show me. "We have fifteen grandchildren. They are our sunshine."

The viejito nods and pulls out his wallet. It's full of pictures, mostly school portraits. I can tell they're arranged from oldest to youngest child. The butterfly girl is one of the youngest. As I draw, she runs over to check my progress and then runs off again, flitting, just like the butterflies she likes so much. The old couple tells me about their grandchildren—who's good at school, who's bad at school, who plays the guitar, and who's the star pitcher for the baseball team. Since the viejita mentioned sunshine, I draw them in a field of fifteen sunflowers, writing the names of their grandchildren in the veins of the leaves.

"Muchas gracias," the lady says, and instead of one dollar, they give me two, insisting on paying for the young girl's portrait as well.

Five dollars to go, I think to myself.

Luckily, the old couple tells a dog-walker about me. He comes over for a portrait of his bulldog. Then a couple of boys all sweaty from playing basketball stop by. I think they just want an excuse to rest in the shade, but I don't care as long as they pay me.

Just a few more sketches to get me enough money. I'm back to calling out, trying to get people's attention, but they're back to ignoring me. This gig is tough, but I can't give up, not when I'm so close to my goal.

Finally, a construction worker approaches. I can tell he's proud of his body by his tight shirt and the way he struts. "Can you draw me?" he asks. "It's for my girl-friend."

"Sure," I say. He's the first person who actually strikes a pose, putting his hands on his hips like he's Superman, so I add a cape and a Superman *S* to his hard hat.

When I hand over the sketch, he says, "Great job! My girlfriend's going to love this!"

He gives me a ten, and when I start to hand back change, he waves me off. "You've been working hard," he says, "so you deserve an extra tip."

"Thanks!" I say because the extra money puts me well over my goal of earning seven dollars.

As he walks off, I think about what Ava and Rooster said about the people of Tres Leches, how lots are rude but how there are a few nice people, too. Looks like I just met some of the nice ones.

"Okay, Paco. Let's go find our friends."

He knows exactly where they are, and after they come back, we all return to the pharmacy. When we enter, the cart of salt is near the cash registers, but off to the side. Bonita sees us immediately, and she's pleased.

"Are you ready to make the trade?" she asks. "A purse is a small price to pay for something as beautiful as an aquarium with a clownfish."

"I won't need to trade my purse after all," I say. "I have enough money now." I grab the bills and fan them like a hand of cards, a *winning* hand.

The clerks stare at me. They look surprised but only for a moment. Their faces go stern again, and they offer no congratulations. Meanwhile, Bonita's eyes narrow and she frowns, clenching her lips and smudging her lipstick. I wait, trying my best not to tremble because I can tell she's angry—no, more than angry. *Furious* is a better word. But then she relaxes and offers us a smile, the heart on her lips now smudged.

"Well, if there's anything else you need," she says, "I'm always happy to help." Her words are pleasant, but there's no affection in her voice.

I nod, and then Ava, Rooster, and I hurry out with the salt. There's a wobbly wheel on the shopping cart, but we don't care.

"Next step," Ava announces, "flying!"

Rooster moans, but I'm as excited as Ava. I might be afraid of water, but at least I don't have acrophobia, the fear of heights. I look up. The clouds are wispy, but soon they'll be dense with rain.

106

OWLS CAN LOVE, TOO

WE HEAD OUT OF town again. When we leave the paved sidewalks and streets, we have to maneuver the shopping cart around rocks and pull out blades of grass stuck in the wheels, but we manage. We're heading to Ava's to get her tools and her flying machine. As it turns out, she lives in a gigantic oak tree, which, according to her, has been around since before the Alamo.

On the way to the treehouse, Ava shows us her garden. "Here's where I plant the herbs," she says, pointing to plants with labels for rosemary, mint, basil, and oregano. We take a moment to pinch off leaves and sniff. Next, she shows off her xeriscape garden with Texas sage, plumbago, and lantana, and then her cactus garden with a giant nopal full of yellow blooms. "And finally, my pride and joy," she announces, "the vegetable garden!" She's planted rows of carrots, onions, and corn. There are wire cages supporting her tomatoes, and trellises for her green beans. She has all kinds of peppers and squash, and she even has watermelons and strawberries. Paco grabs a strawberry and takes a bite.

"My mom is a strict carnivore," Ava explains, "so I have to grow my own food."

She then leads us to her tree. It's majestic. The tallest tree in Tres Leches by far—the trunk too wide to hug, the branches and leaves casting a large circle of shade. At the base is a rope ladder that leads to a portal above. The opening is small, too small for my backpack, so I set it down.

Rooster also sets down his boom box but not because he's going to climb. He sits and makes himself comfortable by leaning against the tree. "I'll watch the salt."

"Thanks, Rooster," Ava says, and to me, she whispers, "My mother hates salt."

"Why?"

"It makes her feel weak."

I guess her mom has high blood pressure because I heard that too much salt can make that condition worse.

Before we grab the ladder, Ava puts a finger to her lips and says, "Shhh. My mother's sleeping."

I nod, and then we make our way up; I'm a bit wobbly on the ladder till I find my rhythm. I follow Ava through the opening and find myself in a circular room with the tree trunk in the middle. Dozens of extension cords run along the floor. They're connected to all kinds of lamps—floor lamps, table lamps, lava lamps, lamps hanging on chains from the ceiling, and lamps clipped to the tables and shelves. There are plenty of windows, but it must get very dark at night. Then again, Ava can see in the dark, so the lamps don't really make sense.

"My room's on the top level," she says, "but we have to go through my mom's room first. Just be very quiet. She'll get angry if we wake her."

I almost ask if she works the night shift, but then I remember she's a witch, and I can't help wondering . . . does Ava's mom cast spells? Does she cook mice and lizards in a giant cauldron? Does she have green skin and warts?

"Come on," Ava says. She's already a few more steps up the ladder. I follow. Right before she disappears into the next opening, she puts a finger to her lips, a reminder to be quiet, and then she disappears into the darkness above.

I try my best to be silent, but it's hard. I'm a little out of breath, so I'm making scuffling sounds. Soon it's my turn to slip into a room with no windows. It takes a moment for my eyes to adjust. Luckily, some light filters in through the cracks in the walls. I should be climbing, but I'm too curious. I search for a cauldron or broom, but there's only a web of extension cords attached to more lamps, and then . . . a shadow along the far wall. At first, I think it's a bed, but it's not. It's . . . it's . . . a giant nest! And in the nest is Ava's mom—it must be!

I feel a tug on the rope, and when I look up, Ava's urging me forward, so I start climbing again.

As soon as I'm through the next portal, I whisper, "Was that your mom?"

"Yes," she whispers back. "Step softly. These floors are creaky." I have a million questions, but Ava doesn't give me a chance to ask. "Welcome to my room-slash-study-slash-workshop," she says.

It's exactly as she described it. Like the rooms below, the space is donut-shaped, with a tree trunk in the middle. I step carefully to avoid tripping over more extension cords, connected to even more lamps. There's a bed and a wardrobe, but the rest of the room is devoted to flight. The walls are full of diagrams for flying machines, giant blueprints that Ava must have drawn herself, but also pages ripped from books and magazines. She has a table saw, a sewing machine, and a workbench. Scattered on the floor are scraps of wood, twine, feathers, and fabric, the kind used for kites. She even has a pile of assorted wheels, castoffs from bicycles, wheelbarrows, and lawn mowers. Her single bookshelf is filled with books about birds.

"So I'm guessing you want to be a pilot someday?" I say, teasing.

"Yes, and no," she answers, surprising me. "I want to fly but not only in planes. I want to *be* the plane. Actually, I want to be a bird, to use my own muscles to get up there. But if that doesn't work, then being a pilot is my second choice."

Ava's room has windows, but since we're in a tree, it's very shady. Not a single lamp is switched on. She tiptoes to a sheet draped over something that's as tall as us.

"And now," she announces, "my latest invention and the answer to seeding the clouds." She grabs a corner of the sheet and, with a dramatic flourish, yanks it free, revealing a pair of wings. "I designed them myself," she says. "For the frame, I used balsa wood, the same wood used for toy airplanes. Then I glued netting to the frame and sewed feathers onto the netting. It took over a month to find enough feathers, even with Paco's help. He's an expert scavenger." She points at the different feathers as she identifies them. "Mockingbird, pigeon, blue jay, crow, and owl."

"Wow," I say as I circle the wings, inspecting. "This is impressive."

It must have taken tons of patience to make. The feathers are perfectly aligned, each hand-sewn onto the frame. She's even added straps to attach the wings to her arms.

"We'll lower them from the windows."

At first I'm thinking that we're going to toss them out, but when we get to the window, I discover a pulley. Ava goes "Pssst!" to get Rooster's attention. Then she loops the wing straps through a hook and very carefully lowers them to the ground, where Rooster unhooks them, giving us a thumbs-up when he's done.

"And now for my tool belt," she says, "in case I need to make adjustments."

She grabs a leather tool belt and buckles it around her waist. I never thought I'd see a girl wearing a tool belt, dark goggles, and a blouse with embroidered flowers. I'm definitely going to draw her portrait soon. Maybe I can give it to her as a thank-you gift.

She reminds me to be quiet again, and then she heads down. I follow, but going down is trickier than going up. The moment I enter her mother's dark room, my foot misses a ladder rung, and I panic, scrambling to find it. My hands start to get rope burns as I slip, but I still can't find that rung! My feet scrape against the tree trunk, the frantic movement swinging the rope. "Hold still!" Ava says in a harsh whisper. At that moment, I find my footing again, but it's too late. The rope's still swinging. Ava slams into the tree, and a wrench falls off her belt, clanging when it hits the floor. She freezes, and so do I.

I grip the rope tightly as I try to catch my breath. The shadows swirl around, making me dizzy. For a moment, I'm confused. *Which way is up, and which is down?* Luckily, I get my bearings again, remembering that I'm in a giant treehouse with Ava and that we're frozen because of a clang that might have woken her mother—her mother, who's a witch!

I hear something behind me—a soft rustling—perhaps a blanket being pushed aside. I turn toward the sound, clenching the rope even tighter and biting down on my lip to keep my noisy breath inside. The shadowy figure moves. Ava's mother is awake! I squint at her because it's so dark. Most of her face is covered, but one eye peers back at me. It's huge and round like Ava's—like an owl's! A glowing ring of orange surrounds the pupil, making the eye look like a solar eclipse.

It blinks, and I gasp, caught between amazed and afraid.

"Sorry, Mom," Ava says. "We're leaving, so you can go back to sleep."

Her mother doesn't answer. She blinks again and then ducks back into her giant nest.

My next steps are very quiet and very slow. I remember one of Reynaldo's rules—if you see a giant owl, hide. I'm not sure if Ava's mom is an actual owl, but she's certainly owl-*like*. I *don't* want to wake her again. I hold my breath until we leave the treehouse.

"What took you so long?" Rooster asks.

"We accidentally woke my mother."

His eyes go wide.

"It's okay," Ava says. "I thought she'd hoot and screech, but she just went back to sleep."

Now that we're safely outside, I have to ask. "So your

mother is an owl? An actual owl? Because Reynaldo told me to hide if I ever see one."

Ava nods. "They call her La Lechuza, and she's only an owl at night."

"But how? And do you become an owl at night, too?" The questions pour out of me even as Rooster shakes his head, warning me to stop.

"No," Ava says. "I do not become an owl. Do you become a ghost when you get near water?"

I shake my head to answer.

"So why would I become an owl at night, and why would Rooster become a devil?"

"I didn't say anything about Roo—"

"We don't get to pick our relatives," Ava interrupts. "I wish my mom weren't an owl-witch, but she is and she's still my mom. We don't see eye to eye on a lot of things, but we still love each other. And before you ask, yes, owls can love, too."

With that, she stomps off, Paco close behind.

"I didn't mean to upset her," I tell Rooster. "I mean, my mom's a ghost, so I get it."

"No, you don't," Rooster replies. "You're new here. The town doesn't even know that you're La Llorona's daughter. You haven't experienced what it's like to be related to a monster."

I don't respond, because he's right. I just learned about my mom yesterday, so I haven't lived with the truth for very long. In fact, I've been so eager to meet her that I haven't processed what it means to have a mother who's a ghost. Then again, a part of me agrees with Reynaldo about keeping my identity a secret. Without realizing it, I've been afraid to let people know for fear of being shunned, bullied, and blamed just like these new friends of mine.

I run to catch up to Ava. "I'm sorry," I say. "I didn't mean to upset you."

She just shrugs.

After a few more steps, I say, "I don't care what the town thinks about you or your mom. *I* think you're interesting. You're the first person I've met who knows a lot about famous pilots and planes. And I really admire those wings you built."

She smiles, but just a little bit.

"Do you forgive me?" I ask. "Can we be friends?"

She doesn't slow her steps or turn toward me, but she does manage to say, "Sure. I guess."

Right now, that's good enough for me. We walk a little farther, but then we hear Rooster. "I could use a little help here," he calls. He's added his boom box, my backpack, and the giant wings to the shopping cart, everything piled high. He can barely see where he's going. Ava grabs one wing, and I grab the other, lightening the cart. Soon, we're on our way again. Sometimes Paco runs beside us, and sometimes he runs ahead or leaps from branch to branch. Apparently, we're looking for the perfect tree.

"How about this one?" I say, pointing to a tree with gold blooms.

"The huizache? Too short," Ava answers. "Besides, those thorns will rip my wings."

"How about that one?" I nod toward another tree, this one with white flowers.

"Taller, but the anacua is not tall enough."

Rooster steps in front of Ava, blocking her path. "I don't think jumping off a tree is a good idea. You're going to break an arm or a leg if you jump from too high."

"Paco jumps off trees all the time," Ava says. At this, Paco flicks his tail. "Besides," she adds, stepping around Rooster, "it's a great idea. My best idea so far."

"That's what you said when we built the giant ramp."

"And at that time, the ramp *was* my best idea. But this one is even better."

Rooster shakes his head. "I just think—"

"Don't be such a party pooper," Ava says. "It's going to work. I promise. Remember that story we read?"

"How could I forget? It's all you've been talking about."

"What story?" I ask.

They give me a recap of a Greek myth about a man named Daedalus and his son, Icarus. In the story, a king had trapped them in a giant labyrinth that Daedalus had designed. To escape, Daedalus made wings, using wax to secure the feathers. He warned his son, "Don't fly too close to the sun or the wax will melt." They climbed to a high window and jumped off. The wings worked, but of course, Icarus ignored his father's warning. He flew too close to the sun, the wax melted, and he fell and drowned in the sea, more proof that water is dangerous.

"Ever since reading the story," Ava says, "all I can think about is the wings."

"All *I* can think about," Rooster counters, "is the drowning boy. The story is supposed to be a lesson about not aiming for something you can't do and about listening to your elders."

"Do *you* listen to *your* elders like your father?"

"I would if he weren't such a devil."

"In my mind," Ava says, "the story is telling us that making wings out of wax is a dumb idea. I mean, seriously, of course they're going to melt. Thus"—she turns over a wing to show the stitching—"I did not use wax."

"She's got a good point," I say.

"But you could break an arm or a leg," Rooster warns again, "or suffer a concussion. Or worse, you could break your back."

Ava looks dreamily at the clouds. "*Best*-case scenario? I fly."

Rooster sighs. "You never listen to me. No one ever listens."

"I listen to you *sometimes*," she teases, already running away, Paco close behind.

Rooster and I speed up to catch them, but the shopping cart hits a rock and now the wheel keeps swerving to the left. It takes two of us—me pulling and Rooster pushing—to get it moving in a straight line.

"Look!" Ava says. "It's the perfect tree!"

She's pointing at a pecan tree as tall and majestic as the oak with her treehouse. It's probably been around since before the Alamo, too.

"What a perfect launchpad," she says.

"Or diving board," Rooster adds, "and there's only one direction from a diving board. And in case you're wondering, that direction is down."

"It's a launchpad." Ava insists. "There's only one direction from a launchpad, and in case *you're* wondering, that direction is up."

As if to prove her point, Paco rushes ahead and scurries up the trunk.

We all follow. When we get to the top, Ava sets down her wings and circles the trunk, her fingers lightly skimming the bark. Then she studies the branches.

"I'll climb to that branch right there," she tells us, pointing to one that's broad and straight, "and, Rooster, you can hand me the wings. I'll climb to that higher one while you catch up. Then you'll hand me the wings again. Felice, it's your job to give me the salt. We'll have to use your backpack, and it'll probably take several trips. But no worries. Very soon, we'll be making it rain." She removes her tool belt and adjusts her goggles while I replace the items in my backpack with salt.

"We should at least have a trampoline or a giant mattress, something to break your fall," Rooster says.

"I am *not* going to fall," she insists, grabbing hold of the tree and lifting herself.

After she gets to the first branch, Rooster hands her the wings. They follow the plan, Ava climbing to the higher branch and Rooster handing her the wings again. Then I climb with the salt. When I reach her, I hand over the backpack, which she places against her tummy, and I hold the wings as she slips her arms through, making sure they're strapped securely. It's a little tricky, but we manage. Once she's ready, Rooster and I climb back down to give her room. Then she takes a deep breath and jumps.

She doesn't fall as Rooster predicted, but she doesn't fly, either. Instead, she glides a few feet and gently descends, landing with a soft thud.

Rooster runs over to check on her. "I told you it wouldn't work," he says.

"What are you talking about? It *totally* worked!"

"If that's true, then why are you on the ground?"

Ava hands us the wings and the backpack full of salt and returns to the tree. "I forgot to flap," she explains.

"In order to fly, I must flap my wings. I can't believe I forgot such a basic action."

Paco is still on the tree, eating a pecan. He barks in agreement, a few crumbs falling out of his mouth.

Ava climbs again, beckoning Rooster to hand her the wings and follow. For a second time, I give her the salt and help with the attachments. She takes a deep breath like before and does a few shoulder rolls. Then she jumps, this time flapping her arms. She's in the air for two or three seconds longer, but once again she hits the ground.

"Did you see that?" she asks us. "I actually flew that time!"

"You did!" I cheer. "You were in the air for at least three seconds."

"I'm not sure that was flying," Rooster says.

"I just have to flap faster. Like a hummingbird. I have to be a hummingbird!"

"They're very tiny, and you're not," Rooster says, but Ava isn't listening. She's already at the tree again. She pets Paco when she reaches him. Then she tells Rooster and me to hurry.

"It's going to work this time," she says. "I can *feel* it."

I can feel it, too. It's going to work this time. It *has* to!

We repeat the process. This time after strapping on the wings, Ava takes *two* deep breaths, rolls her shoulders, *and* wriggles her fingers. She runs a few steps on the branch before jumping. As soon as she's in the air, she flaps as if she were a hummingbird, but it's not graceful or coordinated. One wing lifts faster than the other, so now she's twirling through the air and then . . . twirling toward the ground! Instead of landing with a soft thud, she lands with a few heavy bumps, then skids along, leaving a trail of feathers and salt behind.

When she finally comes to a stop, Ava calls for help. "Rooster! Paco! Felice!"

We run over. "Are you hurt?" Rooster says. "Did you break an arm or a leg? Did you snap your back?"

Ava has her eyes closed, and she's trying her best to shield her face with what's left of her wings.

"My goggles! I lost my goggles! I can't see!"

"Don't worry," Rooster says. "I'll find them."

He retraces her path, searching. Finally, he spots them. They're dusty and a bit scratched but otherwise okay. He hands them to her, and when she puts them back on, he helps her up. She leaves the wings on the ground and dusts off the dirt. Then Rooster grabs her in a formal dancing pose and leads her in a few polka steps.

"What's this for?" she laughs as she follows along.

"We're celebrating your survival."

"I'm fine, Rooster. More than fine. I can walk. I can dance. I can *fly*!"

Rooster lets go, stopping the polka mid-step. "What

are you talking about? That was the *opposite* of flying. You need to face reality, Ava. Those wings won't work. Tell her, Felice."

I don't want to admit it, but he's right.

"Are you kidding?" Ava says. "They work great! It's my arms that don't work." She scans the ground for fallen feathers. Paco has already collected some and made a little pile.

"Thank you, buddy," she says.

"You're going to try this crazy idea again?" Rooster asks.

"Yes, after I lift weights and swim and do a bunch of push-ups. Then I'll be strong enough. Then I'll fly for miles. But"—she looks at me—"I'm afraid I won't be able to do this any time soon."

Before the disappointment settles in, we hear a loud roar, and when we turn toward the sound, there's a giant cloud of dust.

"El Cucuy!" Rooster cheers.

Sure enough, it's Reynaldo. We wave and whistle to get his attention. He honks the horn in response, and when he reaches us, he hops off his truck. He's all out of breath, as if he ran instead of driving over.

"There you are!" he says to me. "I've been looking everywhere for you. You're never going to believe what Bonita did!"

IT'S NOT EXACTLY OPERATIONAL

I THOUGHT REYNALDO HAD something new to report, but he's only repeating what we already know—Bonita has dried up the river to run off La Llorona in exchange for the bakers' tres leches recipes.

There aren't any breaks in his story, so we let him talk on. "And did you also know that for the bakers, pan dulce no longer tastes sweet, honeysuckle no longer smells sweet, and besos from their hijos no longer *feel* sweet? Can you imagine a kiss that is nothing more than a spot of slobber on the cheek? And all because of Bonita." He clenches his fists, and then, with extreme effort, relaxes them. "The bakers have shut their stores. They wander around, feeling useless, watching as everyone goes to the pharmacy for cake. It's a horrible way to live—your very life purpose snatched away. And yet!—this is most tragic of all—the bakers do not blame Bonita for their misery. Instead, they praise her for getting rid of La Llorona and making them feel safe. But at what cost? There's no river. There's no sweetness. Bonita takes more than she gives, yet her popularity soars!" At this, he lifts his arms, and I almost expect him to soar, too, but just as quickly, his shoulders slump again. "I'm going to lose the election," he moans, "after *one* term! After all the improvements I've made and the ones I announced for the future. And to think that I will never see my vision fully realized and all because of"—he pauses and then snarls—"Bonita!"

I'm depressed by all this bad news. I glance at Ava and Rooster. They look depressed, too. Even Paco has lowered his head. I hurt for Reynaldo, who wants to be mayor not because he's power-hungry, but because he loves his town even though it's full of gossipy, whiny, and ungrateful people. But—and I know this sounds selfish—I hurt for myself even more. I ran away from Uncle Clem, the one person who supported me all these years. It's true that he kept me from knowing that my mother is a ghost, but only because he thought he was protecting me. I can't help feeling mad, but at least I can understand his actions. Still, I don't regret running away, because more than anything, I want to meet my mom. Person or ghost, I don't care. I've come so close to seeing her, so I can't give up now. I have to believe—I *do* believe—that I can overcome any obstacle. One thing is for sure: Nothing is going to happen if we just stand around feeling sorry for ourselves.

"Come on, guys," I say. "Cheer up. We have a plan. We just have to make it happen."

Reynaldo perks up. "You have a plan? What is it?"

"Bring the river back by making it rain," I say. "All we have to do is seed the clouds with salt. We have the salt"—I point at the shopping cart—"but we're struggling to reach the clouds."

"I tried flying, but it didn't work," Ava admits.

Reynaldo stoops down, picks up a feather, and examines the scene for the first time. I can tell he's imagining our attempts.

"And you believe this will work?" he asks.

"Yes, it's based on science," I explain. "I learned about it in school."

"Aha!" Reynaldo says. "I can get behind science. I actually prefer it. If only our town felt the same, for both science and magic have consequences. In the words of Sir Isaac Newton, one of the greatest scientists of all time, 'For every action, there is an equal and opposite reaction.' The difference between science and magic, however, is that with science, you can predict the consequences, but with magic, you cannot." He looks at the clouds and squints at the sky. "We will seed the clouds, my friends!"

"But we can't fly," Ava reminds us. "Not yet, anyway."

"On that point, I must correct you," Reynaldo says. "For not only do I have El Cucuy, my monster truck, but I also have Lil' Cucuy, my monster plane."

"You have a plane?" Rooster asks.

"Yes, but before you get too excited, you should know it's not exactly operational."

Ava's already grabbing her tool belt. "Not a problem. If there's one thing I know how to fix, it's a plane."

So we pile into the monster truck, glad to have a break from walking.

Reynaldo takes us to an airstrip with several small planes in a hangar. I recognize Lil' Cucuy right away because of its paint job—fangs and menacing eyes on the nose, flames on the wings and tail, and claws on the wheel covers.

Reynaldo parks beside it. We all jump down, Ava rushing over. "A Cessna TTx!" she announces excitedly. She circles the plane, her fingers lightly brushing its surface. "Three-blade, constant speed propeller. Fixed landing gear. Straight wings with a span of . . . hmm . . . thirty-six feet? Seating for four. Fuselage-mounted tail unit." She spots a couple of ladders leaning against the back wall of the hangar. "Help me with those ladders so we can remove the cowling," she tells Rooster and Reynaldo. They follow her directions, lifting the engine cover after Ava unscrews the bolts. Then she's peering at the engine, muttering to herself the whole time. "Six-cylinder, fuel-injected, twin-turbocharged engine." She grabs tools. From my vantage point, I can't see what she's doing, but she looks very busy. She wipes sweat off her forehead, leaving a smudge of grease, and then, "Aha!" She pulls something out, shows it to us. It looks like a rusty metal thing. "Hose clamp," she says. "Totally ruined, but easy to replace." She tosses it to Reynaldo. "Go grab a new one."

"I'll be right back," he announces.

He goes to the workbenches, toolboxes, and supply cabinets lined against the walls and rummages around. After a few minutes, he holds up a shiny new hose clamp and delivers it to Ava. She reaches into the engine again, grabbing tools to make adjustments. Then she checks the oil level for good measure, and once she's satisfied, she asks for help again, this time to replace the engine cover.

"Good as new!" she announces. "Let's fly!"

"Uh, are you sure?" Rooster says.

"What's wrong?" Ava replies accusingly. "You don't trust me?"

"I trust you. I'm just not sure I trust that plane. What if we're up in the sky and it goes caput?"

Paco chimes in, too, spreading his arms to mime flying, then making choking sounds, then following up with a big show of crashing.

"Your uncle would never forgive me if something happened to you," Reynaldo says to me.

"But we have to go! We have to try!"

"I'm with Felice," Ava announces, opening the door to climb into the cockpit.

"Of course," Reynaldo says, "but as a precaution, we must take parachutes." He rummages around again, finds four parachutes, and gives a quick demonstration on what to do in case we need to bail out.

Finally, we get back to our task, loading the bags of salt and climbing in. Rooster and I take the back seats while Ava and Reynaldo sit up front. I can't tell who's the pilot and who's the copilot because they're both flipping switches and turning knobs. Paco's not with us. Instead, he's on the runway, holding orange wands and using them to guide the plane. First, he makes a quick circle with his right wand to tell us to start the engines, then raises his left wand to signal a left turn, and then uses both wands to urge us forward.

Finally, we're at the airstrip. "Seat belts!" Reynaldo orders.

I double-check mine. It's secure and tight.

"I'm good," I say.

"Me too," adds Rooster.

Ava gives a thumbs-up.

Reynaldo takes a deep breath. He and Ava look at each other and nod. We're ready to go.

And we're off, racing down the airstrip, but not like a meteor, more like a stone skipping across a pond, catching air, then hitting the surface before catching air again. The end of the airstrip is fast approaching. I close my eyes and brace for the impact because I'm positive we're going to run right into the trees, but then a few more bumps and we're up, rising, just grazing the tree-tops.

"Whoa!" I say.

"Woo-hoo!" Ava cheers.

Rooster's just laughing. I can tell he's as excited as we are.

But it isn't smooth soaring, more like a roller coaster with sudden dips, the kind that make my stomach jump to my throat. Rooster and I gasp, grab the armrests, close and then open our eyes, not sure we want to see what's happening but unable to resist looking. The plane turns suddenly, and the centrifugal force pushes me toward the center. A bolt rattles across the floor. Where did it come from? Shouldn't it be holding the plane together? I glance around, half-expecting the wings to fall apart.

We roll, heading downward, the ground getting closer. Rooster and I scream. No wonder this plane's named after a monster!

I let go of the armrest and grab Rooster's hand, holding on for dear life. Like I said, I'm not afraid of heights, but I am afraid of crashing. Then, inches above the tallest trees, the plane pulls up sharply. We howl, a strange mix of fear and relief. Now instead of the ground, we're facing the sky, shooting up like astronauts in rockets.

"You have to get control!" Ava yells to Reynaldo.

"I'm trying, but I can't remember what all these levers are for!"

She slaps his hands away from the controls and tries her best to level the plane, but it bucks and twists like a bull with a cowboy on its back. We're all frantic, but Ava keeps her calm, mumbling to herself as she takes over flying. Eventually, she levels us off. The engine sputters and coughs for a few moments, but soon it's quietly humming.

"I think I'm going to be sick," Rooster says.

"Barf bag is behind my seat," Reynaldo tells us.

I reach into the pocket behind his seat and pull out a bag, then hand it to Rooster. He opens it, but luckily he doesn't throw up. I don't want to stare, so I glance down, Tres Leches shrinking as we rise. From up here, I can see the long arroyo that marks the dried-up river. Rooster leans back, takes a few deep breaths, one hand on his stomach as if to keep it calm.

"Feeling better?" I ask.

He nods.

"Sorry, guys," Reynaldo says. "It's been a while since I've flown, and it took me a minute to find the magic touch."

What is he talking about? He's not the one with the magic touch. Ava's in control now, and every time Reynaldo reaches for something, she gives him a warning look.

So he gives up, clasps his hands behind his head, and surveys the scene. "Flight," he begins, "once the domain of birds, bats, and mosquitoes, but now also of humans, whose ingenuity and perseverance have resulted in wonders of engineering such as this, a plane—but also rockets and spaceships, for we have set our feet on the moon, our robots on Mars, and our—"

"We're here!" Ava announces. "Altitude: twenty-five hundred feet."

We're right in the middle of a puffy cumulous cloud, surrounded by white mist with occasional patches that let us glimpse the ground.

"No time to waste," Ava says.

That's our signal. Rooster, Reynaldo, and I get to work. First step is to put me into a harness that's secured to the plane just in case I lose my footing. I've also got Reynaldo holding the straps.

"Don't worry. I won't let you fall," he says.

But I'm not worried. I'm excited to be so far above the ground. I completely understand why Ava wants to fly. In Tres Leches, people are sometimes mean. They quickly judge others like Ava, forgetting that she's smart, nice, and helpful if you just give her a chance. But up here, it's quiet. The loudest insults can't rise this high. No one can touch you, and even though it's dangerous—I can fall at any moment—it also feels safe. Plus, from up here, Tres Leches is so small, which makes the problems down there feel small, too.

I take a moment to enjoy the peace, but when Reynaldo asks if I'm ready, I'm jolted back to my mission and give him a thumbs-up.

He and Rooster open the door. The sudden rush of wind makes Reynaldo's braid whip around and the plane lurch a bit, but Ava quickly regains control. I lean out, Reynaldo firmly gripping the straps. Rooster hands me the first bag of salt. I open it and pour, but some of the salt flies back inside.

I take a few steps closer to the edge. "I need to lean out farther!" I shout over the sounds of the engine and the wind.

"It's too dangerous," Rooster warns. "We should head back."

"No, let's try again," Reynaldo says.

"Just give me the next bag," I tell Rooster. "No way am I turning back now."

He shakes his head but reluctantly hands me the second bag, and this time, all the salt flies into the clouds. After a few more tries, we have a rhythm, Rooster handing over the next bag as soon as I've emptied the previous one. Eventually we're all out. Reynaldo reaches into a pocket and gives me three little packages of salt, the kind you get with to-go orders of papas con huevos taquitos. I tear them open and dump the contents. Next, we sweep out whatever salt fell back into the plane, so now we're *completely* out. Not a grain of salt anywhere. I don't know if we gave enough to seed the clouds, but at least we tried our best.

We return to our seats, and once we're buckled in again, Ava takes us back to the airstrip—no bumps on the landing, no screeching to a stop. That girl can fly!

When we exit the plane, we all glance at the puffy cumulous clouds. It's hard to believe we were actually there, up so high. The clouds slowly change shape as they drift across the sky, but there's no other difference. They're still white, not gray like rainclouds.

"What now?" Rooster asks.

Ava and Reynaldo scratch their heads. I'm puzzled, too, trying my best to remember all the details of my classmate's cloud-seeding presentation.

"The next step," I say with fake confidence because I'm not sure but I *have* to believe, "the next step, my friends, is to wait."

7UP USED TO BE CALLED *BIB-LABEL LITHIATED LEMON-LIME SODA*

SINCE WE HAVE NOTHING to do while waiting for the cloud seeding to result in rain, Reynaldo suggests we go to the Mesquite Bean Inn. "You're going to love Lulu," he says.

I glance at Ava and Rooster. They're nodding.

"She makes the most delicious mesquite bean jelly," Rooster says, rubbing his stomach.

"I *am* kinda hungry," I admit, because my slice of cake was hours ago, and my breakfast was a couple of hours before that.

"It's settled, then," Reynaldo says as we climb into El Cucuy. "Next stop: the Mesquite Bean Inn."

Back in Tres Leches, Main Street is still full of bakers, but they're sitting on curbs or leaning against walls, bored. Instead of sweet pan dulce, the air smells like car exhaust and horse manure. To make matters worse, the REAL-TIME POLLING RESULTS billboard shows that Bonita has a solid six-point lead. Reynaldo shakes his head and tsk-tsks. "She was five points ahead two hours ago," he mutters to himself.

We go past Bonita's Pharmacy and the town square to a section of Main Street I haven't explored yet. That's where I discover El Camarón, the dance hall and arcade that Reynaldo warned me about. Its sign has a picture of a bull-riding cowboy, but instead of a bull, he's on a giant shrimp. The curtains on all the windows are drawn, and there's a CLOSED sign on the door.

Turns out, the Mesquite Bean Inn is right across the street. It's a white two-story building with balconies on the upper floor, light blue shutters around the windows, and saloon doors.

Reynaldo pulls over to park, and when we hop out of the truck, one of the curtains at El Camarón moves aside. I can't see who moved it because it's too dark in there, not even a shadow, but Rooster nods in that direction as if to say, "I see you" or "What's up?" Then the curtain falls back into place.

"Who was that?" I ask.

He looks at me with sad eyes. "My dad."

He doesn't say anything else. I have a dozen questions, but I don't ask them because I remember how Ava felt earlier when I asked about her mom. I don't want to offend my new friends, especially after all they've done to help, but I'm desperate to know more. Maybe, someday soon hopefully, Rooster and Ava will trust me enough to share their stories with me.

"Come, come," Reynaldo urges. "Lulu loves company." He swings open the saloon doors and calls, "Lulu! Lulu!"

Rooster, Ava, Paco, and I follow, a rush of cool air meeting us as we enter a room that is more like a restaurant than a hotel lobby. There are tables with upside-down cowboy hats being used as planters for ivies, the leaves and tendrils spilling over the hat brims and snaking around the table legs. An upright piano and a microphone sit on a small stage beneath a hot-pink neon sign that says LULU'S. A few cats lounge on the steps of a staircase with even more ivies curled around the banister.

"Mayor Reynaldo!" I hear.

I turn to the voice. It's coming from a Black woman... Lulu, I'm guessing. She's standing behind the bar, polishing a glass but setting it down when Reynaldo offers a hug. She has long white hair braided into cornrows. Instead of a necklace, she wears a whistle on a chain.

"Lulu," Reynaldo says, "meet Felice." He waves me over. "Felice, meet Lulu."

I offer a handshake. "Hello, it's—"

"Have a seat," she says. "You too, Rooster and Ava." She sniffs the air. "Young man, when are you going to start wearing deodorant?"

"I tried," Rooster says, "but it doesn't—"

"Though I can't blame you for *not* wearing it," Lulu says. "All those chemicals. Have you read the ingredients? Aluminum zirconium octachlorohydrex? Stearyl alcohol? Talc? Unnatural, I tell you, and to think what they're doing to your skin, maybe getting absorbed and hunkering somewhere inside your body, waiting for the moment to strike you sick. You go on stinking, hon. At least you'll be alive to keep turning noses."

Reynaldo taps the counter with his piñata stick. "How about some drinks, Lulu?"

"Oh, pardon me," Lulu says, laughing at herself. "What kind of bartender forgets to offer drinks?" She points at herself. "My kind, I guess." She follows this up with a strong "Ha!" Then she puts shot glasses in front of us, and Reynaldo makes a big show of clearing his throat, his way of reminding her that we're minors who can't enjoy tequila shots. So she goes to a freezer and pulls out frosty mugs. "Root beer for everyone!" she announces.

Reynaldo clears his throat again. "You can give them root beer, but I'll have a *beer* beer, thank you."

She uses a bottle opener to pull off the caps and pours, the fizz bubbling just over the tops of the mugs without dripping down the sides. For Reynaldo's beer, she manages to pour a fizz-free glass.

And the whole time, she's talking.

"It's called *root beer* because the original recipe got its flavor from the sassafras root. It was actually a tea, originally. Calling it *beer* was a marketing ploy to make it more appealing to all those tired workers. But it's genius, isn't it? Changing the name made all the difference. Then again, 'What's in a name?' I believe Shakespeare's Juliet said that, and apparently, the answer is *everything*. Consider—microwaves used to be called *radar ovens*, and Google used to be called *Backrub*, and 7UP used to be called *Bib-Label Lithiated Lemon-Lime Soda*. I myself am Lulu for short, but my real name is Louisa Lillibeth Lawrence. A mouthful, I tell you. A mouthful! Can you imagine the mayor stepping in and instead of 'Lulu, Lulu,' calling out 'Louisa Lillibeth Lawrence! Louisa Lillibeth Lawrence!'? Knots up the tongue, don't it? And speaking of names, honey, what's yours again?" She's looking at me, but before I can answer, she says, "Ah yes, it's Felice. I do believe you're the first Felice I've ever met, and I've met lots of people."

While she talks, she toasts bread, spreads mesquite bean jelly on the slices, and piles them on a plate, letting us grab as many as we like. I try thanking her, but she never gives me a chance. She's too busy listing all the people she's met and following each name with an anecdote. It's a very long list, and the anecdotes are more like novels than little stories. Reynaldo seems riveted by every word, but after the last slice of bread, Ava and

Rooster slip off their barstools. They find a table in the back and start their own conversation. I want to join them, but that would be rude. Then again, Lulu hasn't really noticed that they're gone.

"And you, Reynaldo? How are you doing?" she asks.

"Well, the election—" he begins.

"I'm sure the election is upmost on your mind," she interrupts. "If I were running for mayor, I'd be thinking on it every minute of every day. From a voter's perspective, there are so many pros and cons to consider. For example, you have accomplished some wonderful things. The bell peppers in the street are just delightful. So what if a few cars have suffered dings from swerving around them? A few *more* cars were getting flats when there were potholes. On the flip side, however, are all the *other* streets that still have potholes. I know there are only so many hours in the day but— Ah yes! You fixed the town clock! I set my watch to it every time I pass by, for my watch is always out of sync. And to think that some people blame the clock for all their late appointments. Excuses, I tell you. Excuses! Not to mention how you helped me remodel the inn. Planting ivies in old cowboy hats is genius."

"I do like to watch things grow."

"I want to vote for you, Reynaldo. I really do, but—and don't take this personally—but it's you against *Bonita*."

"She's—"

"A formidable opponent, I agree. After all, she's the pharmacist! She might be a bit rude, but think of all the problems she's already solving—stomachaches and ear-aches and headaches. Stuffy noses and bad backs. Broken bones and broken hearts. Not to mention what she did for *me*."

"What did she do for you?" I ask.

"Oh, sweetheart, before I went to Bonita, this place was swarming. A person in every chair and barstool, and everyone talking at once, telling me their problems but never asking how *I* feel, never listening to *me*. I was an ear. That's all! An ear. And a hand, I guess, since I was constantly refilling their drinks and taking their cash."

"But isn't that a good—" Before I can finish, she's back to the election.

"I honestly don't know who I'm going to vote for," she tells Reynaldo. "On this side, you." She holds out her right hand. "On this side, Bonita." She holds out her left. "Both of you are my friends. I almost wish a stranger were running as well. That's who I'd vote for, so it wouldn't seem like I was taking sides, but take a side I must, for that is the very nature of a vote. It's an expression of your preference, so I must consider the issues, not my friendships, first."

"Well," Reynaldo says, "I have some ideas for—"

"Of course you do. I've always admired your ideas. Especially the one about—"

140

At that moment, I hear a note from the piano. Then another and another. When I glance back, it's Paco, hopping across the keyboard, playing what now sounds like a jazz tune.

"Help us move these tables," Ava says.

She and Rooster are already pushing one aside.

"Music!" Lulu cheers as she hurries to join them.

Reynaldo leaves his piñata stick on the bar, and he and I get to work. Soon, we've cleared space to dance. Rooster doesn't even have to ask. Ava and I are ready, each of us taking one of his hands. Somehow that boy manages to dance with two girls at the same time. We never stumble over each other's feet or lose the rhythm. He's masterful at leading us. A little pressure from his hand or turn from his hip tells us how to move. For this, we're doing a quick one-two-three and then a longer *SWIIING* back.

One-two-three, *SWIIING* back. One-two-three, *SWIIING* back.

Every now and then, I glance at Paco. He looks like he's dancing, too, using all four feet and sometimes his tail to hit the notes. Who knew squirrels could play pianos?

Reynaldo and Lulu also dance. She never runs out of breath, even though she's moving and talking at the same time.

"Used to be," she says, "we had live music every night.

141

Do you remember, Reynaldo? Open-mic sessions. And you never knew who'd show up. Sometimes jazz musicians; other times, country; or the Tejano bands. They—"

They're out of earshot for a while, but when I'm near them again, she's saying, ". . . Mr. Avila with those strange fruit poems."

We're dancing for almost fifteen minutes before Paco hits a sour note. He keeps on playing, but then he hits another sour note. I accidentally step on Rooster and then Ava bumps into me. Reynaldo and Lulu seem to lose their rhythm, too. It takes me a moment to realize that we're all distracted by another sound, faint at first but getting louder—the strong bass notes of a distant band.

Ava gasps. "It's getting dark!" she says, alarmed, and without explanation, she grabs her tool belt and runs out the door, with Paco close behind. They remind me of Cinderella running from the ball when the clock strikes twelve.

Rooster takes a deep breath and says, simply, "El Camarón." Then *he* leaves, too.

Now that it's quieter at Lulu's, I can hear the distant music. It's coming from the dance hall and arcade across the street.

"Why'd they leave?" I ask Reynaldo.

Lulu sighs as if gathering her strength. I wait for her to start another long story, but instead she walks to a back closet, returns with a broom, and starts sweeping.

"Come with me," Reynaldo says, grabbing his piñata stick and leading me outside. He lowers the tailgate of El Cucuy, and we sit there, our legs dangling. At El Camarón across the street, the curtains are still closed, but between the cracks are colorful flashing lights. When people get close to the windows, I see their silhouettes.

Meanwhile, Rooster's in the middle of the street, trying his best to warn off the teens. "Go home," he's saying, and "Stay away from El Camarón," and "It's dangerous here." No one listens. He gets in front of a boy, but it's no use. The boy bumps him in the shoulder. I can tell it hurts because Rooster rubs at the pain. Most kids ignore him, keeping their distance and holding their noses, but some spit at him or push him aside. "You can't tell us what to do," they say.

"That boy," Reynaldo tells me, pointing at Rooster with his piñata stick, "lacks the power to persuade."

"Why is he out there?" I ask. "Why does he care if people dance or play arcade games?"

"It's his burden," Reynaldo explains. "Haven't you noticed, my friend? This town is cursed."

"Because of my mother?"

"Partly. But also because of Rooster's and Ava's families." He nods toward another group of teens heading to El Camarón. "Every night, instead of doing homework or chores or just spending time with their abuelos, the teens of this town party. They're out all night, so they're

143

useless in the morning. Sleeping late and failing classes because they can't concentrate. And some never go home at all. They run away."

"But why is that Rooster's fault?"

"It isn't. Not exactly. But he feels responsible because his parents own the business."

"And Ava?" I ask. "Why'd she run off, too? Is it because her mother's an owl-witch?"

Reynaldo raises his eyebrows, surprised that I know.

"I saw her earlier," I say. "At the treehouse."

He nods. "It's true. And as you know, owls are nocturnal, so Ava's mother patrols the skies at night, looking for people who should be at home and not wandering about. Every night, Ava runs home and tries her best to convince her mother to stay in the tree. She lights lamps, hoping all the light will fool her mother into thinking it's still daytime."

We sit quietly for a while, watching poor Rooster.

"I want to help," I say, scooting forward, but before I can jump down, Reynaldo puts his piñata stick in front of me, an obstacle.

"You *will* help. But first, you must meet your mother. Right now, no one knows who you are, so it's best to keep your identity a secret. Everybody thinks Bonita solved the problem, but drying up the river is not the answer. Your mother must find peace. Once that happens, we will turn our attention to our friends."

He's right. My number one goal is to meet my mother. Still, it's hard to sit here and watch Rooster struggle. Even now, some guy's flapping his arms and going "Cock-a-doodle-doo! Cock-a-doodle-doo!" The girl who's with him walks up to Rooster and says, "I think you need to cool off," as she pours her ICEE on top of his head. He clenches his fists, but instead of fighting or saying something mean, he takes a deep breath and with extreme charm, says, "May I have this dance?"

The girl can't resist. She takes Rooster's hand, and they start to dance a cumbia, since that's what's playing at El Camarón.

"Hey!" the boy calls out. "Come back here!"

But the girl ignores him. She's dancing with Rooster down the street. Looks like she's enjoying herself.

"He'll dance her all the way home," Reynaldo says. "That's how these nights always end—Rooster asking someone to dance and saving at least one person."

We watch until they turn a corner. The crowd thins out soon after, probably because almost everyone's already in the dance hall.

"Mayor Reynaldo," we hear. It's Lulu at the saloon door. "I have to finish telling you my story."

"Yes, my friend. I'll be there in just a sec."

But she doesn't give him a second. She grabs her whistle and blows, the sharp sound hurting my ears. She keeps on blowing like a lifeguard at the pool, and I shudder at the thought of all that water.

"¡Ya voy!" Reynaldo says, but she doesn't stop the whistling till he hops off the tailgate. "I'm on my way, Lulu. Just give me one more sec!"

"You better hurry because it's a very good story," she says before going back inside.

"She's being a bit pushy, isn't she?" I ask.

"Yes, but la pobrecita can't help it. She went to Bonita and traded her corkscrew for that whistle."

"I heard her mention that Bonita is a good friend."

He thinks a moment. "Bonita once had many friends, but now all she has are customers. Lulu's grateful for the whistle, but I wouldn't say that she and Bonita are true friends. Lulu doesn't realize it, but she was better off before, because now, instead of listening to everyone's woes like a good bartender, she uses the whistle to get your attention, anyone's attention, so she can talk and talk and talk. She seems happy, but she's also very lonely because everyone's tired of listening to her, as tired as *she* used to be when listening to *them*." He's walking backward, adjusting his cowboy hat. "I've heard her stories many times over, but I must hear them once again because that's what a real friend does."

Then he's gone, back inside the inn, leaving me on the tailgate with my feet still dangling.

The streetlight buzzes, trying its best to turn on but not quite getting there. I glance at the sky and spot the first stars. I should go inside with Reynaldo and Lulu, but this is the first moment I've had to myself. I can't believe I've been gone the whole day. I thought that by now I would've met my mother and we'd be on our way to Corpus Christi to reunite with Uncle Clem. But tomorrow—tomorrow it's sure to happen.

I smile, imagining my uncle and mother's reunion after so many years. I'm sure Uncle Clem's angry that I ran away, but he'll forgive me once he sees his sister. They'll have so much to talk about, and together they can tell me stories about Henry and Gustavo. I'll finally get to learn about my brothers! I'm sure Mom will always be sad about losing them, but with Uncle Clem and me in her life, she'll begin to heal.

IT'S BETTER THAN NAMING THEM
AFTER SANDWICH MEATS

I STAY ON THE tailgate of El Cucuy for a while longer, thinking about my adventures until—I can't help it—I yawn, fatigue taking over, and it's no wonder, since I've been hiking and dancing my way through Tres Leches County. I've been climbing trees and leaning out of an airplane, too. That's a lot of excitement for one day!

Luckily, I'm at the Mesquite Bean Inn, where I can get a room and sleep. That's my plan, anyway, but before I can hop off the tailgate, the door to El Camarón creaks open.

A man steps out. He's wearing a cowboy hat and a denim jacket over a white shirt. Like most men in Tres Leches, his belt has a giant buckle, this one with a rhinestone-studded picture of the dance hall's logo, the cowboy "bull-riding" on a shrimp. This must be Rooster's dad, I realize, the owner of El Camarón.

When he notices me, he tips his hat to say hello, and my cheeks get hot from blushing because he's the hand-somest man I've ever seen.

I watch, mesmerized, as he reaches into his pocket for a cigarette and puts it between his lips. Then he snaps, and a fire ignites from his fingertip. He lights the cigarette, takes a few puffs, and blows on his finger to put out the flame. I'm still processing the idea of a fiery finger when I notice something even stranger. His jeans are cut short, revealing his feet, only they're not human—they're like a chicken's. I close my eyes and shake my head, still doubting. Then I look for a second time, and it's true. Rooster's dad has chicken feet!

I should be freaking out—this man just snapped a fire into being and he's not entirely human!—but I'm more curious than scared. Now I understand how Rooster got his name and his good looks. His father is just so *handsome*. So what if he has chicken feet? No one's perfect. And snapping up fires? It's probably just a magic trick. I heard magicians use something called "flash paper" to make that happen.

The music gets even louder, and Rooster's father takes one more puff before snuffing out his cigarette. Then he starts for the door, but before going inside, he glances back at me, jerks his head in a way that says "Come on over." Before I know it, I'm hopping off the tailgate and crossing the street. My steps aren't regular walking steps, they're taps and slides. My hips sway, my shoulders roll, and my fingers snap. I'm dancing! Rooster's dad holds open the door as I approach, and the lights inside are the bright colors of lollipops. There's hip-hop music, and I glimpse some kids break dancing.

I don't bother to glance back at the Mesquite Bean Inn even though Reynaldo's warning is echoing in my mind. *"Don't dance at El Camarón!"* it's saying, but another voice, a louder voice, is telling me it's okay. It's just one dance. Five minutes tops. How dangerous can it be? After all, it's Rooster's dad, and Rooster's my friend. He helps me, so wouldn't his dad be helpful, too?

I hear laughter from the dance hall, and I can't wait to join the fun. I'm just a few steps from the door to El Camarón—one, two, three—and I'm about to cross the threshold when—lightning! Then a long drumroll of thunder. I look at the sky, the moonlight and stars hidden by clouds. A single drop lands on my forehead and like a cold finger taps me awake. I shake my head, coming back to myself.

What was I thinking? I'm not supposed to go dancing at El Camarón. I can't believe I almost broke one of the mayor's rules, but I forgot myself for a moment, just like I forgot myself earlier with the bluebonnets.

Rooster's father is still holding the door open, but instead of forward, I'm stepping back. And it's a good thing, too, because just as I step into Lulu's, the rain pours down.

"We did it!" Reynaldo exclaims. "Science has prevailed!"

His voice sounds so far away because louder than Reynaldo's cheers is the rain and louder than the rain is my heartbeat. My legs want to give out, so I hold on to a table to keep from falling. I'm dry and safe inside, but the rain—it's right there! And one of the things I do—I can't help myself!—is imagine scenarios like a leaky roof or water seeping through the floor, and in all these scenarios is a catastrophic moment like the roof crashing down from the weight of so much water or the floor cracking open to reveal an ocean underneath.

"Dear child, what's wrong?" Lulu asks.

"It's . . . it's raining." That's what my mouth says, but my mind's telling me to breathe in and breathe out. If I don't do it, I'll hold my breath in fear, and at some point, I'll pass out.

"Your plan worked," Reynaldo's saying, impressed. "You made it rain. We'll have a river by morning."

"Now why would you be happy about that river?" Lulu asks, but she doesn't give us a chance to answer. "It's not very impressive as far as rivers go. If it were the Mississippi or Nile or Ganges that disappeared . . . well . . . that'd be another story. Wouldn't want *them* gone. They're majestic. But this river . . . it's got that terrifying ghost that's always crying. La Llorona."

"She's not terrifying," I insist. "She's my—"

Reynaldo shakes his head, giving me a silent warning. He wants me to keep my secret.

"Then again," Lulu goes on, "I suppose every river has its tragic story. I can't think of a single one that hasn't flooded at some point in its history. But *our* river? Our river has the *most* tragic story. That woman was a fool for love. A wedding planner, can you believe it? She planned everybody's wedding but her own. No wonder she drowned—"

"That's enough of this sad story," Reynaldo interrupts because I'm shivering from my fear of water and from my anger at hearing more chisme about my mom. This is the first time I've heard about my mom planning weddings, so I'm angry at Uncle Clem again because he never told me anything about my family.

"Are you cold?" Lulu asks.

"No, I'm . . . I'm . . . afraid."

"Of a little rain?"

"It's not a *little* rain," I say. "Listen." Amazingly, she does. It sounds like pellets from a thousand BB guns are pounding the roof.

"She's afraid of water," Reynaldo explains.

Lulu tilts her head, thinking. "Well, I've got the cure for that. We'll keep you dry, warm, and comfy." She's grabbing my arm as she speaks. "Let's get you settled in a room."

"You can sleep here tonight," Reynaldo says. "Lulu will take care of you. And don't worry about the cost. I've already paid for the room."

Lulu leads me to the stairs, and we start climbing. A

cat is in the way, so she picks him up and gives him a light kiss. "Hello, Mr. Feta." He squirms and jumps from her arms, but there are other cats, and they get lifted and kissed, too. "Hey, Cheddar. And what's up with you, Pepper Jack? Miss Provolone, did you cough up more hairballs today?"

Miss Provolone seems to nod yes.

"Now, you're probably wondering why I named my cats after cheeses," Lulu says. I'm not wondering about anything because I'm still focused on the rain. Climbing stairs with shaky, weak legs isn't easy. "Well, it's better than naming them after sandwich meats," Lulu explains. "That's what I say. Can't have cats named Turkey, Ham, or Bologna running around. Though Salami has a nice ring to it. I was going to name them after automobiles or gemstones or even ice-cream flavors. I still think ice cream would've worked. Mr. Feta *does* look like a Rocky Road, don't you think?"

She's still talking about names for cats when she shows me to my room, and the only reason she changes the subject is because now it's time for my tour. Lulu points out the bed, the armoire, the balcony door, the window, the wallpaper, the restroom, the rug, and on and on. I don't exactly need a tour since the location of everything is obvious, but I can't find a way to end the conversation.

"Lulu! Lulu!" Reynaldo calls from downstairs. "Where did you get this antique cash register?"

She scoffs. "That man has the worst memory. I've told him a dozen times I found it at the flea market." She's shaking her head, but she's only pretending to be annoyed. "You know where I got it," she calls down to him as she leaves the room.

I shut the door behind her and whisper, "Thank you, Reynaldo." I know he can't hear me, but hopefully he can feel my gratitude. Lulu's sweet, but she loves to talk, and right now, I'm too tired and afraid to listen.

I try to get ready for bed, but then the lights flicker and there's another crack of thunder. The window is covered by a sheet of rain, and I tremble when I realize that only a single pane of glass separates me from the water.

I hide beneath the blankets and press two pillows against my ears to mute the storm, but it's no use. I'm warm, dry, and comfy like Lulu promised, but it's not enough to calm me down. When I'm afraid like this, especially when other, *un*afraid people are nearby, I start to feel foolish. After all, no one else seems worried. Many people pray for rain, thank it, and there's a lot of beauty in the way the plants perk up after a good soaking. I try to appreciate the rain, to think of how it's good, but all that comes to mind is the terrible storm that caused my family to drown, so now instead of feeling grateful, I'm even more afraid.

I try breathing techniques and distracting myself by

focusing on other sounds. I even fill a cup with water and stick my finger in it to prove it can't hurt me, but nothing works. If only Uncle Clem was here. He'd know how to help. I should have stayed in Corpus Christi, where it's familiar and safe. For the first time, I'm beginning to believe that coming here was a big mistake.

THEY'RE BURNING EVERYTHING!

THE NEXT MORNING, IT takes me a moment to remember that I'm at the Mesquite Bean Inn. I pull back the blankets, squinting and shielding my eyes from so much brightness because my room faces east and gets the full morning sun. Then again, a sunny morning is a good thing, since it means it's no longer raining. I rush to the balcony. It might have been wet last night, but it's completely dry now. I take a deep breath. The air has that fresh after-rain scent.

I quickly get dressed, grab my purse and backpack, and tiptoe downstairs, trying my best to avoid Lulu because the last thing I need is another long conversation. No sign of her in the lobby, so I sneak outside. The bakeries have reopened. This has to be a good sign! They must have reopened because the river's back.

"Excuse me, sir," I say to the first man passing by. "Do you happen to know if the river has returned?"

"Of course it's returned. What do you expect after a thunderstorm like the one we had last night? I hate living near a cursed river with that whiny ghost crying all the time."

"But maybe if she stops crying, then you could return to the river," I say.

"Want to know what I think?" he asks. "Those bakers betrayed the town and somehow made it rain because they wanted their recipes back. And for what? They should have stayed closed. They're burning everything!"

I sniff the air. He's right. Instead of smelling sweet pan dulce, I smell charred bread.

"So now," he goes on, "we have a cursed river but nothing sweet to comfort ourselves, and it's all because of those selfish bakers!"

With that, he stomps off. I don't bother telling him it's my fault because my friends and I are the ones who made it rain. I hate the idea of everyone being angry at the bakers, but if I share what really happened, they'll probably arrest me, and I can't meet my mother if I'm in a jail cell. Plus, these people don't need more reasons to bully Ava and Rooster or to vote for Bonita instead of Reynaldo. The townspeople might be angry right now, but as soon as my mother meets me and stops crying, they'll be happy again. They'll return to the river, and they'll thank me. They'll thank the mayor, too, and probably the bakers, even though they aren't part of our plan.

I'm about to head into the Mesquite Bean Inn, bracing myself for long-winded Lulu, when El Cucuy comes roaring down the street. Reynaldo takes up three parking spaces again. Then he hops down from the cab of the truck. Instead of twirling his piñata stick, he leans on it like someone who needs a cane to hold himself up.

"What's wrong?" I ask. "You seem disappointed and tired. Aren't you happy that our plan worked? We brought the river back."

"Yes, yes, that's very good, but I thought I'd gain a few points." We glance up at the REAL-TIME POLLING RESULTS billboard. Reynaldo is still trailing behind.

As he speaks, a baker heads over and reaches us just in time to hear Reynaldo complain about the polls. "I'll tell you why you're behind," the baker says. "You broke your promise to fix the river, but at least Bonita was willing to do the job. Only, the river's back by some devilish miracle. And now there's a lot of chisme in town, and everyone's saying it's the bakers' fault because we asked for a refund on the promise, but we didn't. The recipes were back in our shops this morning, so as far as we're concerned, Bonita's playing fair, since her plan didn't work. But it's not doing us any good. We've still got that cursed river, and even after following our recipes, we can't seem to make anything delicious."

Before Reynaldo can say anything in his defense, the man walks off.

"They don't understand," Reynaldo complains. "Now

that the river's back, we can get rid of the curse the correct way, by giving La Llorona some peace. Then they'll get to go fishing and tubing again. Can't they see? Once we free La Llorona, they can have their tres leches cake and eat it, too."

I try to cheer him up. "Look on the bright side. The first part of our plan worked, so the second part is bound to work, too. And it's all because of you and your genius idea of bringing me here."

"It was genius, wasn't it?" he says with a weak smile.

Before I can continue, a group of people runs by, glancing back as if they're being chased.

"It's coming! It's coming!" they yell at us. "Run! Hide! Save yourselves!"

I glance down the street. All seems normal until another group runs by and yells at us, too. Right after they're gone, Ava, Rooster, and Paco emerge from the alley where they were hiding from the crowd.

"Do you know what's happening?" I ask.

Rooster answers, "Mr. Canales heard from Mrs. Brenner, who heard from Mrs. Nguyen, that there's a new monstruo approaching. It's just outside of town, but it's headed this way."

"What kind of monstruo?" Reynaldo asks.

"Depends on who you ask," Rooster says.

To prove his point, three girls on go-carts skid to a

stop in front of us. The first one says, "Mr. Mayor, have you heard the news? A blob's heading to town. It's swallowing everything!"

"It's not a blob," the second girl says. "It's a giant slug that leaves sticky slime as it crawls. People are getting stuck in it."

"That's not what I heard," the third one says. "I heard it's a fudge monstruo. Or maybe it was a sludge monstruo."

The other girls laugh at her. "You don't know what you're talking about. You're just hungry." Then they hit the gas and zoom off, leaving the third girl behind. "Wait for me!" she calls as she chases them.

Reynaldo taps his piñata stick on the ground. "It seems we awakened two monstruos with the rain last night."

Just then, a vaquero on a horse pulls up. He's heading in the same direction as the townspeople, but he isn't running, and he doesn't seem afraid even though his muddy boots and lasso tell me he's been on an adventure. When he reaches us, he tips his cowboy hat at Reynaldo to acknowledge him.

"Oigan," the vaquero says. "Ya viene un monstruo." He nods to the street behind him.

"What kind of monstruo?" Reynaldo asks again. "A blob, a slug, or a mass of fudge?"

"N'ombre. It's made of mud."

"You've seen it with your own eyes?"

The vaquero nods. Then he shakes his muddy boots and holds up his muddy lasso to confirm.

"So you tried to capture it?" Reynaldo guesses.

"Sí, pero no pude."

After a moment, he saunters off, the frightened townspeople sprinting past him.

"Must not be a dangerous monstruo," Rooster observes. "He's the only one who's actually seen it, and he isn't in a hurry to get away."

"It's probably not a monster at all," Ava says. "You know how this town is, always jumping to conclusions."

"Yes, yes," Reynaldo says. "Perhaps this—let's call it a stranger—is more nuisance than threat. Or perhaps it's just a lost creature." He's not leaning on his piñata stick anymore. He's holding it up, his way of announcing an announcement. "I, Mayor Reynaldo Martínez de la Peña, must solve this mystery for the good of my community. Instead of running away, I will venture toward the unknown, possibly putting myself and my legacy in jeopardy. Fear not, for I do this selflessly and for the benefit of my people even as my ratings dip in the polls. As an elected civil servant, I care more for my people than my popularity, and for this reason, I will continue to serve them till the last second of the last minute of the last hour of my term . . ." He takes a deep breath before continuing. "And till my final breath on this most beautiful earth." He reflects on his promise for a moment, then opens El Cucuy's door.

"Wait a minute!" I cry. "What about my mother?"

"You are in good hands," Reynaldo says. "El Cucuy and I will seek out this mud monstruo, while you three"— Paco flicks his tail and barks—"perdónenme. While you *four* search for La Llorona."

With that, he hops into his monster truck and turns the ignition, the exhaust clouding the air. His three-point turn is actually a six-point turn because the truck's so big, but eventually he's off, heading toward the outskirts of town.

I'm feeling abandoned, but then Paco jumps on my shoulder and Ava lightly grabs one of my elbows. Rooster zips inside the Mesquite Bean Inn to grab his boom box, perches it on his shoulder, and with his free hand lightly grabs my other elbow. I smile, feeling safe with my friends.

This is the moment. It's finally time to head to the river and meet my mom. I gather my courage and say, "Let's go."

WHAT'S WANDERLUST IF YOU HAVE NO MEANS BY WHICH TO WANDER?

AVA AND ROOSTER START leading me to the river, and I quickly realize that we're going in the same direction as yesterday.

I clear my throat to get their attention. "Shouldn't we find another path? If we don't, we'll get stuck in the bluebonnet field again, and according to my uncle, it's foolish to repeat an action and expect a new result."

"Very true," Rooster says. "Like when Ava kept jumping off that tree expecting to fly."

"I did fly," she says, "but only for two seconds."

"Problem is," Rooster goes on, "we don't know another path to the river."

We stand around, thinking. No one speaks, and I can only imagine what's running through their minds. Maybe they're thinking about how to avoid the magical bluebonnet field—blindfolds and nose plugs to protect against the magic, or full-on sprints to outrun it? Or maybe they're mentally reviewing the lay of the land, the full course of the river and other dirt roads that turn into other kinds of fields. What we need, I realize, is a map.

"Reynaldo mentioned a cartographer," I say. "Maybe he can give us a map."

Rooster and Ava groan.

"So it's a *bad* idea to see the cartographer?" I say.

"Not if you want a map," Rooster replies.

"Or a giant headache," Ava adds.

Then, after a long sigh, they lead me to the cartographer's. This time, we don't have to take back alleys or detours because the streets are empty, everyone hiding from the mud monstruo.

We turn into Esperanza Lane. It probably got its name from the dozens of esperanza plants lining the street. Their bright yellow flowers bob with the breeze, and the petals at my feet remind me of the yellow brick road from *The Wizard of Oz*. The flowers are beautiful, so it takes me a while to notice that most of the shops are out of business. Behind the dusty windows are dismantled mannequins and empty shelves. The signs are splintered and faded. Pigeons have pooped all over the sidewalk, and the potholes are like regular potholes, wide and deep, and without the benefit of bell pepper plants. Esperanza is the name of the street, but it also means "hope," which reminds me of something Uncle Clem likes to say: "Don't get your hopes up too high, because everything that goes up must come down." I always thought he was being too negative, but now I wonder if he was right.

"Are you sure the cartographer's open for business?" I ask.

"Trust us," Ava says. "A few days ago, there was a river, then there wasn't, and now there is. He's definitely open for business." And to prove her point, she says, "There," nodding to a storefront across the street, this one not as dusty. The sign in the window says MAPS.

We head over, a little bell jingling as we open the door.

"Hello?" I call, shivering because it's cold in here.

"Be right with you," someone says from a back room.

Along the walls are cubbyholes with rolls of maps. I scan the labels, but instead of naming countries or states, they name things like fire hydrants, bus stops, and "last known locations." There's a large table in the center of the room with pencils, rulers, protractors, and a giant page, its corners pinned down by snow globes from Tokyo, Paris, Moscow, and Houston. I study it. It's titled FOOD TRUCKS.

The cartographer walks in. He's wearing corduroys, a sweater, and a knit hat with a fluffy ball on top. He must be cold, too, since he's blowing on his hands.

"Hello, Sarah," he says, squinting in my direction and then squinting toward Ava, "Hello, Naomi."

"I'm not Sarah," I say.

"And I'm not Naomi."

"No?" he asks. "Susan, Gertrude, Ximena?" Before we can reply, he sniffs the air and waves his hand in front of his nose. "Rooster? I know that's you. Don't deny it." He starts to gag, making a big show of leaning on his knees and heaving. He finally manages to say, "I kindly ask you to leave, young man. Your scent is—" He can't finish because he's gagging and heaving again.

My poor friend. It's not *his* fault he stinks. "Hey!" I say, ready to give this man a piece of my mind, but Rooster stops me.

"It's okay," he says. "I'll wait outside."

After Rooster leaves, the cartographer recovers, almost immediately, which makes me think he was faking the whole time. Then he grabs an air freshener—linen and sky-scented—and sprays it all over the place.

"So you must be Ava," he guesses, but he's squinting at me.

"No, *I'm* Ava," Ava says. "This is my friend Felice. She's new in town."

He walks up to me and gets real close to my face, trying his best to see. "I should have guessed you were new, but to an old man like me, all youngsters look alike."

I shiver again and rub my arms for warmth.

"My apologies for the cold," he says. "Too much heat and humidity ruins the maps."

"That makes sense," I say, remembering visits to the art museum, another very cold place. I step to the table, looking more closely at the snow globes. "Have you been to all these cities?"

He laughs. "What a whimsical child you are! Of course the answer is yes, if you consider the powers of imagination, but if you want a factual answer, then of course the answer is no, since such places exist only in the books we read. Think about it—the impossibility of a place like Paris, with a giant steel tower, or of another place, like Moscow, with snow. I mean—*snow*? What a curious concept. Everyone knows that frozen rain is quite an impossibility, yet someone has imagined it just as someone has imagined dragons and unicorns, and just as someone else has imagined cities like Tokyo and Houston."

"Houston's not imaginary. I've been there plenty of times."

"Of course you have, my dear." He doesn't sound convinced.

"No, really, I've *actually* been there."

I look to Ava for support, but she just twirls a finger by her ear.

"I know it certainly feels that way," he says. "I, too, have been delightfully fooled." He grabs a couple of books from behind a counter. "For example, I've been to New Mexico," he says, holding up *Bless Me, Ultima*, "and Harlem," he continues, holding up a collection of poems by Langston Hughes, "and Manzanar!" For this, he holds up *Farewell to Manzanar*. "I've even been to Hogwarts!"

"Hogwarts isn't a real place," I say.

"I know! I know!" He claps his hands, delighted. "But it feels real, just like all these other places, which brings me back to my original point about the wonderful power of imagination."

I shake my head, confused. Ava was right. I'm starting to get a headache.

"As a cartographer," he goes on, "I must strive for accuracy."

"I can't handle this," Ava whispers, rubbing her temples. Then, to the cartographer, "I'm going to wait outside with Rooster."

"Suit yourself," he says. He makes his way to the table, sits on a stool, and picks up an eraser. "Are you still here, young Felice?"

"Yes."

"Good. Very, very good. As I was saying, being a cartographer is a challenging job because the landscape is forever changing. One day there's a tree, and then Mrs. Chapa chops it down. So the next day, I must remove it from my map of trees and add it to my map of tree *stumps*. Take this example here." He taps the giant page on the table. "It's a map of the food trucks. I have to update it several times a day." He gets to work, leaning over the page, his eyes literally a few inches away as he revises, adding and erasing things before adding something else. "My process," he explains, "is to spend each morning surveying the land. I take copious notes. Sometimes, I sketch what I see."

"I love to sketch, too." I'm excited to have this in common, but he's not interested. He just keeps talking.

"Then I return here, pull out my maps, and note the changes. Did you know that the six of 1506 Green Grove fell off last week? So of course I had to go to my Green Grove map and erase it. Then, two days later, it returned, so I had to take the map and put it back in."

"Seems like a lot of trouble," I say.

"It's no trouble at all. It's my vocation. I'm blessed with perhaps the most important job in the world. Can you imagine the chaos that would have ensued if someone came searching for 1506 Green Grove when, for two days, it was actually 150 Green Grove?"

He gets back to his food truck map and starts erasing the name of a school.

"Wait! Stop!" I say. "That's not a food truck. That's the elementary school."

He leans even closer and squints. "So it is. So it is. These food trucks are hard to keep track of, always moving around. How inconvenient. But thank goodness you're here. Imagine a town without a school."

"Wouldn't the school still be here even if it weren't on the map?"

"You would think so, but I've seen greater things than schools come and go."

He's right, but so am I. Where we're standing, for example, used to be northern Mexico, but now it's part of the southern United States. Same dirt, same arroyos, and in that way, I'm right. But before being Texas and Mexico, this land was called something else. The people who lived here didn't speak English or Spanish, so in that way, the cartographer's right. Greater things than schools come and go, things like whole societies, when you think about it.

He carefully traces over the letters he's just erased. He's working very slowly because he keeps stopping to check his progress.

"Can you see?" I ask. "You seem to squint a lot."

"I see well enough."

"But don't you need glasses? It might make your job easier."

"I once had glasses," he admits, "but they didn't help at all. They actually made life unbearable."

"Maybe you had the wrong prescription."

"No, the prescription was perfect, *too* perfect. I kept gazing at the horizon and wanting to go there. I had a serious case of wanderlust, a *serious* case, but what's wanderlust if you have no means by which to wander, if

170

you have no courage to go beyond the familiar?"

"Wait a minute. But my friend, the mayor, he said you've been all over the world."

"And so I have. I've been north, south, east, west, and all points in between, but that was after I was cured. You see, when I was gravely ill with the wanderlust, I went to the pharmacy and consulted—"

"Bonita?" I guess.

"Yes. You know her? Sometimes she's a little too blunt, but when I told her my problem, she gave me a cure, and all it cost was my glasses."

I seem to remember a pair of glasses in Bonita's cabinet of curios, and then I remember Reynaldo's most important rule—use only money to buy things.

"Traded them for this eraser," the cartographer's saying, "and then the world opened up because, as it turns out, the entire world was right here all along. Right in front of my face!" He claps, full of glee.

I decide he's speaking figuratively, but who knows. I'm quickly learning that in this town, sometimes people say what they mean and other times they speak in riddles, and I get all confused when I try to sort it out.

No matter. I'm not here for his life story. I'm here for a map, so I return to the cubbyholes. "May I?" I ask.

"Be my guest," he says.

I grab a map from the PETS cubbyhole. It's titled DOGS, and it's a detailed sketch of the town, identifying every property that's home to a dog. The same is true of the cat map, the hamster map, and the maps for goldfish, iguanas, and ferrets. In the UTILITIES cubbyhole are maps of the water and gas lines. The TRAFFIC cubbyhole has maps of parking lots and parking meters. There are maps for places to buy shoes and places to buy groceries and places to buy knickknacks or other useless items. The FIELDS cubbyhole has maps for wildflower fields, cotton fields, and soccer fields. Soon, I've discovered the locations of churches, clinics, windmills, and water towers. I have to admit, it's interesting to see a town from so many angles, but there are hundreds of maps here for only one town—Tres Leches, over and over. Nothing else. *Nowhere* else.

"Did you find what you're looking for?" the cartographer asks.

"No, not yet," I say, "but maybe I'm looking in the wrong place. Can you show me the map to the river?"

He scoffs. "The river? I *curse* the river, for the river has cursed me. Yesterday, it didn't exist. It was a mere figment of imagination. Think about it. How ludicrous—yet how wonderfully fantastical—was the idea of a water stream running for miles and miles when everyone knows that the whole world isn't more than twenty miles north to south and no more than thirty miles east to west."

"That might be the dimension of Tres Leches County, but—"

"Tres Leches County is the *only* county because Tres Leches County is the whole wide world!"

"But—"

"No buts," he says. "As I was saying, yesterday the river did not exist and now it does. I had to wake up at an ungodly hour to put the river back into the maps after spending most of yesterday erasing them, for before yesterday, the river was not a figment of imagination but a very real thing." He stops. I can tell he's just now realizing something by the look of recognition on his face. "I should have known!" he says, punching the air. "You and your friends took the river away and then you brought it back, and now you're here to laugh at my expense."

"We aren't! We didn't!" I say, even though this is only half true.

"What did you say your name was? Felice? I can't believe I fell for the idea of a new girl in town, especially when no other town exists. I bet you're Sarah." He squints at me. "Yes, yes, you're Sarah. And you're hanging out with those two even though they're monstruos."

"They're not—"

"Out!" he shouts, pointing in the general direction of the door.

Intimidated, I take a few steps toward the door, deciding that we can go through the bluebonnet field again. Rooster seems immune, so we have a way through it. Then again, waltzing isn't the fastest way to move. It has a box step that means you go sideways as much as forward. Meanwhile, Reynaldo's quickly losing ground in the mayor's race, but more importantly, my mother is still crying for me, looking for me. If she knew I were alive, she wouldn't let some squinty-eyed cartographer keep us apart.

"No," I say. I face the cartographer again, planting my feet and crossing my arms. "I will not leave until I get what I came for. I want a map to the river, a map with a shortcut that avoids the bluebonnet field."

"The bluebonnet field *is* the shortcut," he says.

"A map with a longcut, then. Sometimes you have to walk farther to get somewhere sooner."

"Don't speak riddles to me!" he says, and he's right. I'm speaking in riddles like everybody else in Tres Leches.

"I'll pay," I say, adding, "with money."

"I'm not sure a young girl like you would have enough."

I touch my purse. I've got about three dollars after buying the salt and the shopping cart, and I don't have time to stand at the corner to draw portraits. We have to go to the river right now.

But I will not give up. "Well? Do you have the map I'm looking for?"

"I have every map you could ever imagine," he says, heading to the counter. He pulls out rolls of maps, holds them close to his eyes to read the labels. "No, no, no," he mutters, and finally, "Yes. This will do."

He offers me a map but doesn't let go.

"How much?" I ask.

"How much do you have?"

I laugh. I am *not* falling for that trick again. "You tell me how much it costs first, and I'll see if I can pay."

He squints at me, studying and probably trying his best to guess how much I have.

"That'll be six cents," he says.

"Six cents?" I can't believe my luck.

"Okay, okay. You drive a hard bargain. You can have it for five cents and not a penny more."

"You mean a penny *less*?"

"Well, I *will* be penniless if you pay me with a nickel. Five pennies will be fine, but if you have a nickel, I'll take that, too. Whatever's best for you. Don't go saying I'm unreasonable. My reasonableness is my special advantage and the reason I'm the number one cartographer in Tres Leches, Tejas. That and my ability to maintain very accurate maps. Did you know—"

I can't take it anymore. I slap a nickel on the counter, take the map, and leave, grateful for the hot air outside after being in such a cold shop.

Ava takes one look at me and says, "Need an aspirin?"

"I think I might need two," I say, "but at least I got the map."

LOOKS LIKE WE LOST THE SIGNAL

MY FRIENDS AND I study the map. We'll be reaching the river at a point north of the bluebonnet field but south of the mud expanse. It's a longer distance, but hopefully we can cross more quickly.

As we walk along, I start to wonder again about Rooster, Ava, and their families, but then my thoughts turn to *my* family, how my mother cries for her lost children. I'm not sure I've ever cried for my lost mom. She's always been an idea, not a real person. When I meet my friends' mothers, I study them, trying to figure out which one is most like my mother, but it's impossible. Some moms stay at home, while others work. Some are very strict, but others let their daughters do whatever they want. Uncle Clem knew my mom, so I rely on him a lot, but even he hasn't given me a clear picture. He tells me she was nice, loving, and creative. That's why I can't make sense of what they say around here: that she lures people to the river to drown them, that she tried to drown my brothers and me—on purpose!

"What do you know about my family?" I ask Ava and Rooster.

They glance at each other, then shake their heads as if to say they don't want to talk about it.

"I know about my dad," I quickly add. "I know he's in another town with his wife, that he left my mom alone to raise three children. We don't have a relationship, but he sends me cards now and then, and child-support checks. But what about my mom and my brothers?" When they don't answer, I say, "Please. Don't I have a right to know about them?"

Ava finally responds. "We heard the whole family died, and that includes you."

"And my uncle?"

"There's no uncle in the stories we grew up with," Rooster says. "Your mother was jealous of the other woman and angry at your father for choosing to stay with his wife."

Ava continues the story. "She took her children to the river and drowned them as a way to get back at your dad, but then she was shocked by what she did."

"That's when she turned into un monstruo," Rooster chimes in. "If she couldn't be with her children, then no one could be with *their* children. She drowns anyone who gets close to the river."

"But that's not true," I say. "My uncle told me the

drownings were an accident. My mother lost her life trying to *save* my brothers."

"We're just telling you what we heard," Ava says. "Everyone in town believes this version of the story. That's why they want your mother gone."

All this time, I've been excited about meeting my mother. But now, hearing this, I feel a greater responsibility. I'm not just here to meet my mom or to help Reynaldo with his mission to reverse the river's curse. I'm here to *rescue* my mom, not from drowning—it's too late for that—but from being remembered as a vengeful monstruo.

Ava, Rooster, Paco, and I walk in silence for a while longer. Then I spot crows on the path, pecking at the dirt. When Paco approaches to see what they're eating, they fly away, and Ava looks up at them, full of admiration and a little jealousy.

Eventually, we turn off the main road to find the trailhead for the river. Even though the sign for the trail is behind an overgrown bush, it's easy to spot because the cartographer's map is very accurate. PATH TO RIVER, we read. BEWARE. At this point, Paco plants his feet and crosses his arms to let us know that he's staying right here. I can't blame him after seeing those bones in the riverbed yesterday. The little guy is scared, and he's not the only one. We're still a distance away, so I'm okay right now, but what happens when we get closer? Will I be too afraid to approach? I was really scared last night during the storm. Then again, I got through it. It wasn't easy. I trembled the whole time. Sometimes you just have to push forward, like now, one step at a time. *One step at a time,* I repeat, but even as I try to force myself, my feet freeze.

"Ava? Rooster?" I say. "You know how I'm afraid of water and how it makes me fall apart?"

They nod even though they haven't seen me panic yet.

"Well, maybe Rooster can play some music on his boom box to distract me."

Rooster smiles. "Music coming right up."

He pushes the power button on his boom box. Instead of playing a CD or cassette, he hunts for a radio station, turning the dial past the stations for rock, oldies but goodies, country, and pop, and finally settling on the station for Tejano music. He turns the dial back and forth a few times to get the clearest sound. Then he turns the volume knob all the way to high.

Paco waves goodbye as we head down the path. Lucky for me, the Tejano station's playing all the classics—Freddy Fender, Emilio, La Mafia, and Selena. You can't grow up in Corpus Christi without knowing who they are.

Rooster, Ava, and I walk down the path, swinging to the beat, our hips and shoulders shimmying. Every now and then, Rooster breaks away from us, his feet doing the cumbia. Ava and I clap with the beat as we catch up to him.

I can't help wondering if my mother likes Tejano music. Will she stop crying when she hears it? I have to believe so. After all, it's helping me forget my fear, so maybe it'll help her forget her grief. That's what I'm hoping for, but then the radio starts to sputter on and off, until it finally dies completely. Rooster hits the boom box a few times, trying to restart it, but it's no use.

"Looks like we lost the signal," he says.

Immediately, my smile disappears. My feet are firmly on the ground, yet I have to steady myself because the world is spinning.

Rooster puts a hand on my shoulder. "Don't be afraid. You can do this. Remember, you're not alone."

I take a deep breath and nod. He's right. I've come too far to give up. I can do this, especially with my new friends by my side.

"Let's go," I say.

Instead of thinking of the river, I think of my mother, beautiful in the pictures Uncle Clem has given me. I try to imagine her in a kitchen or garden, a place that's dry and secure, but I keep seeing her above the river, floating as she keeps watch, reaching for every creature that comes near, and crying with greater and greater sorrow as the years pass without her children, and without a friend or brother to comfort her, and the town twisting her story. What a terrible way to live! How angry she must be. I'd feel angry if everyone I loved left me alone when I needed them the most.

I shake my head, trying my best to find happy thoughts about my mother, but it's hard. She's been La Llorona for so long. I suddenly realize how big this task is and fall out of step with my friends as I worry about the heavy responsibility that lies before me. They ask if I'm okay. I nod even though nodding is a lie. Every step is a lie, too, for as much as I want to help my mom, I'm afraid—not only of the river but of failing to save her reputation.

"Are you okay?" my friends ask again.

This time, I don't bother to nod because the path curves, and as soon as we step in the new direction, I hear my mother wailing, "¡Mis hijos! ¿Dónde están mis hijos?"

Two seconds ago, I wanted to meet my mother, to show the town that she's really a good person and that the drownings were a terrible accident, but I can't think past the roaring river. My heartbeat races, and my face gets hot while my hands and feet go cold. The browns and greens of the plants blur into each other like in Monet's impressionist paintings on my calendar. I squint, trying to focus, but I can't. And now I'm struggling to breathe.

I can't take another breath!

I stand here, frozen like an armadillo trying its best to be invisible. I wish I were braver. I can't even see the river yet, but the fear still shoots through me—a hot, eye-watering, gagging fear—like when you bite into a serrano pepper. Every muscle is on fire, and then I break out of my frozen state and run.

"Felice! Wait!" Ava and Rooster call, chasing after me.

But I'm too fast. I've got that chemical in my body, adrenaline, and it's making me stronger and faster as it rushes through my veins like rocket fuel. The trees rustle as I run past, and the dirt I kick up both hides and reveals where I am. My friends' voices fade away because they can't keep up. I don't care. I can't care! I'm running as fast as my legs will go, and I'm not going to slow down till I'm far, far away from that dangerous river.

WHY DID YOU RUN AWAY AND WORRY ME LIKE THAT?

I DON'T STOP RUNNING till I reach Main Street. That's when I start to feel the aches in my arms and legs, the stitch in my side from breathing fast. I readjust the straps of my purse and backpack because they're pinching my shoulders and neck. Then I lean over, hands on my knees, as I try to catch my breath and slow my pulse. I'd been on autopilot, racing back to town without paying attention to my body or the things around me.

All that matters is being safe, and now that I'm safe, I feel . . . well, I *should* feel relieved but . . . I feel like a failure! I was so close to my mom! With a few more steps, I would have seen her. How can I say that I want to meet her, to help her, when I ran away the first chance I got? I'm such a coward for letting my greatest fear push away my greatest wish.

And now, even with the cartographer's map bunched in my hand, I feel lost. I don't know what to do or where to go. Ava and Rooster are probably ashamed of me, thinking I'm a wimp. When Reynaldo finds out that I ran away, he'll be so disappointed, he'll regret the day he met me. But even if my friends don't think those things about me, I do. I'm a failure *and* a coward.

I wander down Main Street, which is even more deserted now. It seems wider without the cars, bicycles, and horses. The shopkeepers have shut their blinds and turned off their lights. All the businesses, not just the bakeries, are closed.

I call out, "Hello! Anybody here?" Only my echo answers. Only my shadow moves. Tres Leches is no longer the sweetest place in Tejas. It's a ghost town.

I keep wandering until a streak of mud on a chimenea catches my attention. I go to it and discover muddy footprints on the sidewalk. I put two and two together. The mud monstruo—it's here! The footprints are easy to spot. So are the muddy handprints on the windows and doorknobs. I'm guessing the monstruo tried to break in. No wonder everyone's hiding. More chimeneas are streaked with mud, and so are benches, bistro tables, and lampposts. Then the trail of mud veers to the right, down a side street. Now the handprints are on a brick wall, and the footprints start to change, becoming more like smudges. The monstruo must've been getting tired, leaning on the wall for support and struggling to lift its feet. Very soon, I realize that I'm right because I spot the creature. It's smaller than I expected, or maybe it just appears that way because it's sitting on the curb, looking like it's about to slump over.

Very cautiously, I approach. I try to be silent, but I trip over a crack in the sidewalk. "Whoa!" I exclaim, startling the monstruo. It looks up and . . . I can't believe this . . . but it's . . . it's . . . *familiar*.

"Uncle Clem?" I say because that's who it looks like, but no, it can't be. My uncle's not a monstruo. He's not made of mud. Then again . . . "Uncle Clem?"

"Felice?" the creature answers.

"It *is* you!" I say because there's no mistaking his voice. I run to him and stoop to give him a giant hug. I don't care if I get dirty. This is Uncle Clem. He's come to Tres Leches to help me, to help my mother!

He smiles, and for a moment, the whites of his eyes and teeth shine bright against the brown mud that covers his entire body.

"I knew you'd come!" I say. "I knew you wouldn't leave me here to face this town alone."

When I pull away, the mud slips off my hands and clothes, puddling at my feet, but Uncle Clem is still covered. I wipe his back and shoulders. I grab a comb from my purse and run it through his hair.

"It's no use," he says. "I've been trying to wipe it off all day. I've used rags and paper towels. Nothing works." He takes a good long look at me as if to check that I'm still in one piece. "Why did you run away and worry me like that?"

"I'm sorry, Uncle Clem."

"I was frantic when I realized you were gone. I dialed your number. Straight to voice mail. I called your friends, but they hadn't seen you since you left school. That's when I went to the car."

"Did you find my note?" I say, worried it might have blown away.

"Yes, I found your note. But what were you thinking? You should never have run away. All kinds of terrible things could have happened."

He's right. I think about the mud expanse and the enchanted bluebonnets and the frightening rain. I think about how there are devils and witches and bullies around. But then I think about how I got to fly and dance and eat delicious cake, and even though there are a lot of mean people, there are some nice ones, too.

"That's true, Uncle Clem, but it's not *all* bad."

He doesn't reply, just continues. "I don't blame you for sneaking out," he's saying. "I blame myself. I should've known that you'd want to find your mother. I should've known that while I was pretending everything was back to normal after Reynaldo left, you were just pretending, too. I should have stayed up all night. I should have watched the door. The last time . . . when

Alegra . . . I just kept thinking that I wasn't fast enough to save her and what if . . . what if . . . what if *you* were in trouble and I wasn't there to help. Running away . . . it's exactly what your mother did all those years ago!"

He wipes his forehead and examines his hand as if suddenly realizing it's covered in mud. Then he takes off his shoe and shakes it, leaving brown splatters on the ground. It doesn't make a difference. He's as muddy as before. With a sigh, he puts his shoe back on.

I hang my head, ashamed. I knew Uncle Clem would be mad at me, but I didn't realize that he'd also be afraid.

"I got in the car and took off," he says. "When I got on the road to Tres Leches, I saw the warning about mud, but I didn't pay attention. Soon, I got stuck. I pressed the gas, but the tires just turned and turned. Then the sun went down, and it started to rain. That's when I felt the car sinking. All of a sudden, I was back in that night, that terrible night at the river when my family was drowning."

My lip quivers because *I* made it rain, which means I also made my uncle relive this tragic memory.

"When I got out of the car to escape, the mud was at my waist, and it only got deeper. At one point, it was shoulder deep. It took all my strength to move through. I lost my footing a few times and went under. That's how I became"—he holds out his arms—"this."

He turns his palms over and back, as if hoping to see

something different than the brown mud that covers them.

"I'm sorry," I say again, my voice choked up. "But at least you're here now."

He shakes his head in disappointment. "And it's just like before. When I got here, no one welcomed me, not even my old friends. They called me a mud monstruo and ran inside the buildings, locking their doors. I knocked on one and then another, but no one answered. Everyone turned away from me, just like they turned away from Alegra."

"I'm sorry," I repeat. I can't say it enough because I feel horrible about causing trouble for Uncle Clem. "I shouldn't have run away. I should've talked to you again. I should have tried harder to tell you how I felt."

He takes my hand. "It's okay, mija. The important thing is that we found each other. We can go home now."

"But—"

"No buts. We can rent a car and drive home."

He's reaching in his pocket, probably searching for his wallet, but all he finds is brown goop. It doesn't matter. If Uncle Clem believes it's time to go home, he'll do everything he can to make it happen. We'll *walk* our way back to Corpus Christi if that's what he decides, so I have to make a decision of my own.

"I can't leave," I say. "I'm not finished. I still need to meet my mom."

He sighs heavily. "Your mother is dead, Felice."

"She's not," I insist. "I went to the river. I heard her. She's crying for me."

"You went to the river? *You?*" He doesn't believe me, and I can't blame him. He's seen my panic attacks more times than I can count.

"I got close," I explain. "Close enough to hear her, but . . . but . . . I couldn't get close enough to see. But now that you're here, we can go together. You can help me. I know that I'll be brave with you by my side. And once Mom knows that I'm okay, once she sees you again, she'll stop haunting the river. She'll join us. We'll be a complete family again."

"We can never be a complete family," he says. "She's a ghost, and ghosts are dangerous."

"Not when they're your mother."

"Especially when they're your mother! That's when it's hardest to resist."

"But you've always said she loved me, so why would she hurt me?"

He rubs his temples as if to smooth out his frustration. "Your mother *did* love you. She had a lot of love in her heart, but La Llorona isn't your mother, not really. She's just what's left of Alegra after that terrible night, and what's left is vengeance and regret."

"But my mother," I insist, "the good parts of my mother, still have to be there! That's why I need to stay, to help her, to show the town that she's not a monster! They say terrible things about her. They say she drowned us on purpose!"

Uncle Clem moans when he hears this, puts his head in his hands as if he's about to cry. Then he manages to calm himself down by using the breathing technique he taught me. "You can't help her," he says sadly. "She's already a ghost. The river's cursed. You'll ... you'll ... fall in again."

"Not if we go together, Uncle Clem. Isn't that what families do? Help each other no matter how dangerous things might be?"

I refuse to give up, but he won't even consider it. He stands and says firmly, "Come on. We're going home, and that's that."

My uncle Clem, the loving version who's taken care of me all these years, seems very far away, and in his place is this mud monstruo who has given up on his sister, on this town. Well, I'm *not* going to give up.

I stand, too, crossing my arms. "Are you going to help me or not?"

He doesn't answer. He just stares at me, stubborn, and I stare back at him, being stubborn, too. When I realize that he isn't going to change his mind, I feel angry—and I mean, really angry. I always thought I'd yell if I ever felt this way, but I don't—I can't—I just stand here, and the softest parts of me—my cheeks and lips—go hard with fury.

That's it, then. I've had enough. I turn my back on Uncle Clem and start to leave. He grabs my elbow. "I can't let you go to the river," he says. "I'm taking you back to Corpus Christi. It's for your own protection."

I jerk my arm away, easily freeing myself because of the slimy mud on his hands. Without another word, I run away. If he won't help me, then I'll have to do this myself.

"Felice! Felice!" he calls out.

I glance back. He's chasing me but he slips, the mud like slippery ice on his shoes.

"It's too dangerous!" he cries.

Maybe he's right, but I don't listen. When it comes to my mother, I can't afford to play it safe. If I do, she'll be stuck as a ghost forever.

My bravery doesn't last long. As soon as I've returned to Main Street, my anger at Uncle Clem turns to despair. I squeeze my eyes shut, trying not to cry. How can he expect me to forget about my mother and return to Corpus Christi? How can he ask me to pretend she's dead even after I've heard her cries? I don't care if she's a ghost. She's still my mother.

I want to meet her, to save her, but how can I when she won't leave the thing I fear the most? I need help from someone other than my uncle. Reynaldo, Rooster, and Ava have tried, but their attempts to help me face water have failed.

I search the street. The whole town fears my uncle, the "mud monstruo," so the street is mostly abandoned. Every place is still closed—every place except one.

You have no other choice, I tell myself as I take one step and then another toward my only hope for help—Bonita's Pharmacy.

HOW LOVELY

WHEN I STEP INTO the pharmacy, I quickly realize that it's also about to close, not because of the mud monstruo but because it's getting late. The men in green aprons are cashing out the registers. The waitress at the soda fountain is stacking chairs up on the counter. A janitor is sweeping the aisles. Half the lights are switched off, making the pharmacy like the sky—bright on one side, dark on the other.

"Excuse me," I say.

My voice startles the waitress. She drops a chair and doesn't bother to pick it up. The janitor stops sweeping, leans on his broom, and stares at me. The men in green aprons offer nothing, not even a shrug.

"Are you still open for business?"

They keep staring, and it's frightening. My mother might be an actual ghost, but in a way, these people are ghosts, too.

I take a step backward, but instead of the door, I bump into a person, and when I turn around—it's Bonita!

"Um . . . sorry. I didn't mean to bother you."

"And yet, you did," she says, trying her best to hide her irritation beneath a sweet tone. "But as the owner of this place and soon-to-be mayor, I aim to please, so tell me . . . how can I help?"

She forces a smile as she waits for me to speak. Meanwhile, her employees get back to work. A few things clatter as they clean up, but Bonita doesn't seem to notice because all her attention is on me.

"Well . . ." I say, but I hesitate, not sure where to begin or that I should even be here.

"Go on," Bonita urges.

At her encouragement, my hesitation slips away, and all I want is to tell her what's wrong. "I've always been afraid of water," I explain. "I can't even drink from an open glass like a normal person. I need a to-go cup with a lid and a straw, and at home—I'm embarrassed to admit this, but—"

"You'd be amazed at all the embarrassing things I've heard," she says, putting a hand on my shoulder.

"Well . . . I'm still using sippy cups like a two-year-old, and all because I don't want to see the water I'm drinking. And like I said before, I'm from Corpus Christi, which is by the ocean, so there's a whole side of town that I avoid, and it's the pretty side of town, the side where all the cool stuff happens, where people fly kites and go windsurfing and catch fish." I stop suddenly, worried that she's caught my lie about setting up an aquarium, but if she has, she keeps it to herself.

"You were saying?" she asks.

And I can't help it. I keep talking. I tell her about all the field trips and parties I've missed, how I make my uncle take ridiculous detours to avoid bridges over water, how I can't even watch swimming or diving events on TV without cringing, how the very sound of splashing is as frightening as a scream. I tell her everything—the panic attacks, the nightmares, the loneliness because no one seems to understand, even those who care about me. They pretend to understand, but they can't because the only way to know what it's like to be *this* afraid, *irrationally* afraid, is to be inside my head and my body and my rapidly beating heart when I'm in the middle of a full-on freak-out. I tell her everything except for the biggest moment—the night my family drowned. Even though it feels good to share my fears, I know that I need to guard this detail, but it's hard. I have to keep swallowing it down. I can feel myself wanting to blurt out the entire story of my family because Bonita is an excellent listener. She's the most excellent listener I've ever met. She still seems slightly annoyed, but she isn't interrupting me. She's just nodding and saying things like "I see" and "Tell me more" and "Uh-huh," while I go on and on, blabbing away like Lulu...

Just. Like. Lulu.

I glance at the curio cabinet and spot the corkscrew, *Lulu's* corkscrew. She was once a good listener, too, but now she can't hear anyone but herself.

"Is there anything more?" Bonita asks.

I shake my head. "I just wish I could cope with this fear."

At that, Bonita takes my elbow and leads me deeper into the pharmacy. "It sounds like you have a terrible case of susto," she's saying. "Luckily, we have a whole aisle devoted to people with this ailment."

I expected to see a regular medicine aisle with pills or herbs, but instead, there are locked cases with all kinds of cositas—matches for nyctophobia, a blindfold for catoptrophobia, a magnifying glass for micropho-bia, and a rock for . . . a rock for aquaphobia?

Bonita points at it. "See how smooth it is?"

I nod.

"It used to have a rough, jagged surface, but then it fell into the river. The flowing water smoothed it, pol-ished it, and made it beautiful, but more importantly, it gave the stone the power to protect you in water."

"How does it work?"

"You hold it in your hand or put it in your pocket. Just having it near gives you protection."

It seems too simple, but I'm still tempted. At this point,

I'll try anything that helps me face water. I've come too far to give up.

"And how much does it cost?" I ask.

"Well now, that's the thing," Bonita says. "You can't *buy* this."

I step back, remembering Reynaldo's most important rule. "But I . . . I . . . I have money. I drew portraits earlier. People paid me."

"No, no, no," Bonita says. "I will give you the stone *if* you give me"—she smiles, but there's a dark edge to it—"your purse."

She asked for my purse once before, so I shouldn't be surprised, but I am. I'm too stunned to speak.

"There are plenty of other purses," Bonita goes on. "Beautiful purses. In fact, we have a shop in town that sells accessories, and Janet, the shopkeeper, can custom-make anything you like. Another purse with a happy face, perhaps?"

I slowly shake my head.

She sighs heavily. "Do you know that I once gave away mis remedios for free?" She looks beyond me, down the aisle, as if seeing into the past. "I was so happy when I learned that I had the gift of healing. I wanted nothing but to help my friends. For the beautiful, I gave amulets made of black stones to protect from mal de ojo. For the anxious, I brushed away negative thoughts with sprigs of rosemary. I gave away lotions to heal sunburns, and vitamin waters for stamina. I rubbed oils into aching necks and shoulders to relieve the pain. I had many, many friends, and I wanted to help them all, but then"—she looks down, a shadow crossing her face—"one night, we had strong winds. A large branch fell onto my porch, blocking my front door. It was too heavy for me to lift, so I asked my friends for help. They made excuses. Then my faucet started to leak. I can heal bodies and spirits, but not leaky faucets. Every plumber I approached was too busy. I asked the seamstress to pick up my hem, and she did, but she charged me! And to think I had cured her arthritis out of the kindness of my heart! I was so generous at first, but time after time, my generosity was not returned. And that's why I no longer do anything for free."

"But I'm not asking you to give it for free," I say. "I have money."

"I will accept only your purse."

I shake my head again and clutch my purse against my chest to protect it.

"Just think," Bonita says wickedly. "You have been afraid of something that's impossible to avoid. Have you considered that you yourself are mostly made of water? It's in your muscles and veins and brain, and if it's in your brain, it's in your thoughts. It's flooding your thoughts right now."

I gulp, and the action reminds me that she's correct. I *am* made of water. I have saliva and spinal fluid and blood. This whole time I've been a vessel for the thing I fear the most!

Should I do it? Should I trade my purse?

My mind races with the possibilities. If I make the trade, I'll no longer be in danger of drowning. It seems like such a far-fetched idea, but I can imagine—I *have* imagined—how it would feel to dip my toe into a cool lake or river and then to step in and pound my hands on the surface to make splashes. More importantly, I've imagined meeting my mother, hugging her, and telling her my whole life story, every detail, the good and the bad. But right next to these possibilities are the consequences, the very good consequence of helping my mother but also the bad consequence of losing my happy face emoji purse. Even if I get another, this one is very special—it was a gift from Uncle Clem. He said he bought it because I'm always smiling. He's the one who first unzipped it, threw out the tissue from inside, and looped it over my shoulder. It's been my purse ever since. Then again, it's just a purse. There are probably thousands like it in stores.

I shake my head, wishing I had more time to decide,

but so many people I love are in trouble. Reynaldo's about to lose the election, Uncle Clem's a mud monstruo, and my mom's still crying for her children.

Bonita crosses her arms and taps her foot as she gets more and more impatient. She was so kind while listening to me earlier, but I can tell she's going to kick me out if I don't act soon.

"Okay," I blurt before I can stop myself. "I'll do it. I don't want to fear water for another minute."

"Wise choice," she says, reaching into her coat pocket to grab a key ring. She unlocks the case and slides open the panel. "Here we are." She offers the stone. I'm about to take it when she closes her hand over it. She clears her throat and nods at my purse.

"Oh," I say. "Of course." I remove the strap from my shoulder, and the moment I give her the purse, she gives me the stone. It's heavy in my hand. I turn it over and rub its smooth surface. Then I slip it into my pocket, right next to the newspaper article about my family. I do an emotion check. I don't feel suddenly brave. I'm just the same old me.

"I have the perfect spot for this in my curio cabinet," Bonita says. I follow her to the front of the store. Another key opens the cabinet, and she pushes aside a wedding band and dog collar on a center shelf to make room for my purse. She places it carefully, adjusting it so that the happy face emoji is upright and visible. "How lovely," she mutters to herself. Then she closes the cabinet door, and when the lock clicks shut, something inside me clicks, too.

On the surface, nothing's changed, but beneath the surface, everything is different. The pharmacy, for example. It's so clean—the floor and windows sparkle, the shelves are dust-free, and the items are arranged in straight rows—but like a hospital, it's full of germs—millions of invisible germs on the gleaming surfaces. And Bonita—her lipstick, eyeliner, and brows are perfect. There isn't a single strand of hair out of place or a single wrinkle on her clothes or forehead. She's beautiful, but like a figure from a wax museum, one that looks lifelike instead of actually alive.

"This has been such a pleasant visit," she says. "You are the most delightful child."

Even though I see how fake she is, I catch myself blushing at the compliment and say, "Thank you."

"You're quite welcome," she says. "I would love to chat some more, but I'm afraid our business hours are over. And"—she pauses and smiles—"I have to prepare for the mayoral debate tomorrow." At that, one of the green-aproned men holds open the door and Bonita leads me to it. "It's time for you to go, but please, por favor, come back soon."

"Oh, I will," I catch myself saying, and I mean it. Even though Bonita's like a fake wax figure, she's very charming and makes me smile.

I step outside and notice that the sun has slipped beneath the horizon. It's orange to the west, but the east is a dark purple. Soon the entire sky will be black. I need to hurry. It'll be dark soon, and I've a long way to go before reaching the river.

WAAAAAH!

I RETRACE MY STEPS from earlier today, expecting Rooster and Ava to appear from behind a tree or call out for me. It's nearly dark now, so Rooster's probably in front of El Camarón, urging people to go away, and Ava's probably at the treehouse, urging her mom to stay home. I regret leaving them. I could really use their company right now, not to mention Ava's superior night vision, because without a flashlight, I can barely see the path. At least there's moonlight.

I walk along, identifying landmarks. Here's the spot where Paco waited. Here's the path where we listened to Tejano music, and here . . . here's where the trail curves toward the river.

Without hesitating or glancing over my shoulder, I step into the curve, surprised by my new confidence. The stone must be working. I reach for it inside my pocket and rub the smooth surface.

Even though Lulu and the cartographer praised Bonita for her cures, I still thought I'd be worried about water, but knowing I won't drown gives me courage. A day ago—this afternoon, even!—my knees would have buckled at this very spot. I would have curled into a ball, hands over my ears, because I can hear the river more clearly now, but I'm still moving forward.

Then I hear my mother, Alegra—no, La Llorona!—and just like in my dreams, she's crying for her children. "¡Mis hijos! ¿Dónde están mis hijos?"

Her question is followed by a wail, the most horrible sound I've ever heard. "Waaaaah!" The force of it bends the trees. I cover my ears because the high pitch hurts. "Waaaaah!" she cries again, holding the cry for several minutes. Then it's silent.

I remove my hands from my ears, and that's when I hear her again. Instead of wailing, she's sobbing. Every now and then, she moans. "No! Oh no! No, no, no, no!" And then, "¡Mis hijos! ¡Mis hijos! ¿Dónde están mis hijos?" She moans again and cries out, "¡¿Dónde están?!"

Something scurries by, and then something else brushes past my legs. I squint to get a better look. The ground is alive with possums, rats, armadillos, and skunks all heading to the river. Squirrels jump from tree to tree, and bats dart through the air.

"¡Mis hijos!" my mother continues to cry, and then I hear a splash, followed by another and another. The animals! They're answering her call!

"No, don't!" I shout as I hear the shrieks and yelps of

creatures being carried away. "Don't go to the river! She's not calling for you! She's calling for *me*!"

I don't waste another minute. I join the animals and run with them. So many are rushing toward my mother's voice! Now I understand why the river's banned. My mother's wails are frightening but also strangely alluring. These creatures feel *compelled*, just as I felt compelled to stop at the bluebonnet field and step into El Camarón. That's what curses do. They make you forget your better judgment and lure you into danger.

Finally, I break through the trees, skidding to a stop an inch from the river. And now, seeing it for the first time, that fast current, I tremble with fear. Why am I still afraid, especially when I know that the water can't harm me?

Before I can answer my own question, my mother appears, and all other thoughts get pushed aside because this is why I'm here. She's floating above the water, glowing white and wearing a long dress with bell-shaped sleeves. The hem is tattered, revealing her feet. They're twisted and arthritic, and so are the hands covering her face as she sobs. Her hair sticks up in all directions like a hundred spikes around her head. This is not the mother I imagined, nowhere near the beautiful woman from the pictures Uncle Clem has saved.

"Mom?" I try, my voice a whisper.

She moves her hands from her face and wails. "Waaaaah!" The sound bends the trees again and forces up a huge wave in the river, but that's not as frightening as her face, which is wrinkled and scarred by anger and grief. There are bags under her eyes, and her eyebrows form a sharp, angry *V*. "Waaaaah!"

It's the most terrifying sound, worse than thunder and rain, but that doesn't stop the animals. They're still running toward it, jumping in the river, letting the water carry them away as they struggle to swim.

"Mom!" I say again, this time finding my voice and shouting. "Mom! Mom! It's me. Your daughter, Felice!" I wave my arms to get her attention, and I cry out again. "Mom! Mom! It's me! I'm your daughter!"

She stops wailing and turns to me, silently studying my face.

"It's me," I say. "I'm Felice. I didn't drown. I lived."

It takes her a moment to understand what I'm saying.

"¿Mija?" Her voice. It's so hoarse, probably from all those years of wailing. Rocks don't speak, but if they did, this is what they'd sound like. "Is it really you?"

"Yes," I answer. "It's me."

She wipes the tears from her face, blinks a few times, and studies me. "Many have come here," she says. "Many have tried to fool me into thinking they are my children. Many have laughed at my misery."

She looks over my shoulder as if expecting a taunting audience.

"I came alone. I'm your child. Don't you remember having a daughter named Felice?" I reach in my pocket, not for the stone but for the newspaper article. "Gustavo and Henry were my brothers." I hold up the picture so she can see.

She floats over to me. I shiver because she's so hideous, but I will not abandon her. I will not flinch as she gets closer. She reads the headline. "Clemente. Mi hermanito. He saved you?"

"Yes, he pulled me from the river."

"And your brothers?" she asks, hopeful even though the headline clearly states they drowned.

I shake my head to let her know they didn't survive. Her shoulders slump as the horrible truth sets in. "My boys. My poor, poor boys." She repeats this, each time getting louder and closer to wailing again. She's slipping into that horrible memory.

"Mom. Mom!" I say, snapping my fingers to bring her back to this moment. "*I'm* here now. It's horrible that your sons are gone, but you're not alone anymore. Your daughter is alive."

"Felice?" She reaches for my face as she asks the question. It takes all my power to resist stepping back because I'm so afraid. Maybe Uncle Clem is right and she's nothing but regret and grief. But no, I will not turn away, because I love her, no matter what. And then . . . And then she's touching my face, but I can't feel it. Of course I can't. She's a ghost!

"¿Mija?" she repeats.

I nod. "It's me, your daughter." I look her straight in the eyes. "I'm alive."

She tries to smile, but her lips can only tremble. She's been frowning for so long. No matter how hard she tries, she just can't smile yet.

"I've missed you," I say. "I've missed you my whole life."

At that, my mother holds out her arms, and I reach for them, desperately wanting that embrace, and because I forget that she's made of air, I pass *through* her. I can't stop myself. I fall into the river, just like Uncle Clem predicted, and the current sweeps me away.

"Help! Help!" I cry. "I can't swim!"

My mother chases me, trying her best to grab hold. I reach for her, our arms making contact, but it's no use. I can't touch a ghost!

"No! No, no, noooo!" she cries, the wrinkles cutting deeper into her face. "I can't lose you. Not again. Not again!" My poor mother! For the second time, she's failing to save her child. She's probably remembering the night my brothers drowned, the night she lost me and her life. No matter how hard she tries, there's nothing she can do.

My worst nightmare is coming true! I'm deep in the thing I fear the most. The river takes me farther and farther away, past the point where I should have drowned. And far, far beyond that, the whole time, my mother following and grasping at me with her ghostly hands. Then again, I'm not drowning, though I should be. I've been underwater long enough, but I'm still holding my breath. How am I holding my breath? It must be the magic stone!

But my mother doesn't know I'm protected. "Waaaaah!" she cries, forcing up another huge wave in the river. It lifts me and slams me down. My mother's hands clutch at me, and I can't tell if they want to pull me out or push me under.

I fight against the current, trying my best to stay on the surface, but soon I'm too exhausted. I've got nothing left, so I just give in, waiting for a chance to emerge. Sometimes, I'm more than a foot underwater. Other times, a few inches. Sometimes, the river spits me out, giving me a chance to gasp before it swallows me up again. These moments are even more terrifying because when my mother sees me reach the surface, she tries even harder to grab me and gets even angrier when she fails. My back, hips, and shoulders begin to throb after banging against stones and logs and whatever else is in the river. I'm sure my shirt and jeans are torn, but I can't worry about that right now. I've been in this river for who knows how long, and still my mother's wailing.

We grapple through the night, my flesh-and-blood arms with her ghostly ones trying their best to take hold. I don't know what time it is or how long I've been here. I look through my mother's transparent body, searching for the moon, but if it's there, it's beyond the trees. It occurs to me . . . if I can never drown and if my mother can never pull me out, then we'll be locked in this river forever. I'm supposed to bring her peace, but there's nothing peaceful about her haggard face, her desperate attempts to save me. I don't know what to do. I don't know how to help her.

Uncle Clem! I know he can't hear my thoughts, but maybe he can feel them. *Help me! Tell me what to do!*

I don't know if he's sending me a telepathic message or if my memory is grabbing his voice, but I hear him and he's saying, *"Sometimes you have to help yourself first."*

How many times has Uncle Clem told me this? When I shared his belief with Reynaldo at the restaurant, I thought Uncle Clem was being selfish, but now I understand. Not always, but sometimes, you have to save yourself because if you don't, you won't have the power to save anybody else.

My mother can't pull me from the river. She'll never be able to save me. I have to do it myself.

I'm not sure where to start. All I know is that I've been facing up and floating backward all this time. I can see my mother but not where I'm going. Like a turtle on its back, I wriggle, trying to roll over. The current is strong, holding me down, but it's also twisting and turning. It can help me if I let it. Instead of fighting against the current, I move with it. I curl into a ball and let the current roll me over, but now I'm floating feetfirst. I try again and again and finally come out of the roll at the right point so that I'm facing forward, headfirst.

"Waaaaah!" my mother cries.

The huge wave she creates lifts me again, then presses me down. My elbows and knees bump into rocks on the riverbed. That's how deep I'm under. On instinct, I start kicking, trying my best to break the surface, but the current is a strong hand holding me down. I don't panic because I still have Bonita's stone. I can do this. I know I can.

I keep kicking and at the same time use my arms to sweep aside the water. Little by little, the current weakens, and I get control. I look up and see the rippling glow of my mother. It's getting closer and brighter. I'm finally rising to the surface! One last push and my head comes up. I gasp for air, and at the same time, my mother cries again, "Waaaaah!"

"I'm okay!" I shout. "I'm not drowning!"

But I'm not exactly swimming, either. I'm kicking and

churning with my arms, barely keeping to the surface. I get a few mouthfuls of river water and taste the dirt in it.

"Noooo!" my mother sobs. "No, no, no, no, no!"

She'll never believe I'm safe, not until I'm back on land. So I try my best to swim by imitating the moves I've seen on TV, kicking and lifting my arms for some free strokes. I'm not very graceful, but at least I'm moving. I turn, swimming perpendicular to the current. It's still pushing me downstream, but I'm getting closer to land. Then I hit a shallow spot. A tangle of branches is in my way, but it's okay. I'm able to gather my strength and stand. The water's only knee-deep here. I can walk in it now. One step . . . two . . . three . . . and a few more until I'm finally at the riverbank! I fall to my knees, exhausted. I crawl forward, and when I'm a safe distance from the water, I collapse, panting after holding my breath for so long.

I have to rest and let myself get back to normal. A few minutes later, I'm calm again, so I sit up, facing my mother, who's before me, waiting.

"¿Mija?" she says.

Instead of answering, I reach for a hug. I still can't touch her, but it doesn't matter. She's near, and she's saying, "No llores. Todo está bien," because now *I'm* a llorona, my whole body shaking with sobs. I'm so happy to finally be with her, but I'm also regretting all the years we've lost, and I'm sad, too, deeply sad about my family's tragedy, and angry that my father left us and that the town gossiped about it and spread rumors about my mother drowning us on purpose.

I've met her. I've finally met her, but when I release myself from our embrace, I see that I haven't cured her; she's still a ghost.

I CAN'T BELIEVE IT'S REALLY YOU

FOR THE LONGEST TIME, my mother and I sit quietly, recovering from our time in the river. Her glowing form casts a soft spotlight on the water. The way it moves—its curves and splashes—I want to capture it. I've sketched so many still lifes, but I could never sketch a still life of the river because it's always moving.

I reach in my pocket for Bonita's stone. It's solid, the shape unchanging. At first, I think it's the opposite of the river, but then I remember Bonita telling me that the stone once had jagged edges and that the water made it smooth. It might take a very long time, but like rivers, stones change, too.

My mother reaches for me. I place my hand in hers, and together we tuck my hair behind my ear. Once again, she tries to smile, but it's still too difficult. At least she isn't wailing, but she still looks like un monstruo.

"I can't believe it's really you," she says in her raspy voice. "All these years, I thought you were dead along with your brothers. Oh! I shouldn't have gone to the river that night."

"Why *did* you go?" I ask her. "I've heard different stories."

She looks at me as if to ask what I've heard.

"Uncle Clem says you were heartbroken, that you left in search of my father, but the town says you were angry and drowned us in an act of revenge."

She tries to take my hand, but since it's not possible, we settle for our hands resting beside each other in the grass.

"I *was* angry, but I could never be so cruel. I can't believe the town says those terrible things, calling me La Llorona. They forget that I was *Alegra* first. Bringing people together has always been important to me. Did you know that I had a little business, planning weddings and quinceañeras?"

I nod.

"It wasn't easy," she goes on, "when there were a dozen different opinions about food or decorations, but I had a special talent for helping people find common ground. I loved it. That's how I met your father, Andrés. He was a guest at one of the weddings I organized, and he kept asking me to dance. My friends warned me, telling me to stay away from him because we didn't know his people. I didn't listen. Eventually, Gustavo and Henry were born. Then *you* were born, and that's when things started to change."

"That's when he left?" I ask, guessing.

"Your father never really settled in Tres Leches. His home was across the river. He kept promising to marry me, but the proposal never came. The more I insisted, the longer he stayed away. Sometimes weeks would go by. I pretended nothing was wrong. I took on more and more clients to fill my days, but it was hard to be happy about other people's weddings."

She pauses to remember. I can only imagine how it must have felt to plan others' weddings but never your own.

"What man would abandon his children?" my mother goes on. "It didn't seem possible, so at first I blamed myself. But then I blamed him. How could he leave me to be a single mother, to do everything without his help?

"I tried talking to my friends, but they either said I told you so or gave each other knowing glances as if leaving me out of a private joke. I tried talking to my brother, but he was too angry to listen. 'If I ever see that man . . .' he'd say, leaving me to imagine a fight between two people I loved.

"I was not La Llorona—not yet—but I was no longer smiling. How *could* I when my friends turned away from me like I was sour fruit? When clients stopped calling because they were superstitious and didn't want my bad luck to rub off on them?

"Then the chisme, the rumor, that the whole time

he was married to another woman, someone from his home across the river, someone with lots of money. That's why he would never leave her. Everything they said was true, but the *way* they said it—with delight at my foolish actions.

"Then, one night, it started to rain. You and your brothers cried, frightened by the thunder and lightning. That's when I decided to do something. Maybe I didn't need Andrés because I could support myself. But my children . . . my dear children deserved a father.

"When your uncle says I was heartbroken, that part is true, and when the town says I was angry, that part is also true. My heartache and anger mixed together and made me act without thinking. I grabbed you and your brothers and ran toward the river with one goal in mind—to cross it to find your father and make him remember his duty. I had crossed the river many times before, and the water was never more than waist deep, so I didn't think twice about jumping in. I imagined it was shallow, but the rain—all that rain!—it made the river deep and quick. Soon after I stepped in, I lost my footing, the current sweeping me under. I held you tight. You were an infant! And I reached for your brothers. As we tumbled in the water, rocks bruised our arms and legs. When we found the air, we gasped, but there was no relief. The low-hanging branches scratched our faces before we sank again. I tried holding all of you, rescuing you, but there was too much water."

I imagine it. I *remember* it, and I start to tremble.

"So that's when you became La Llorona?" I ask, wanting more of her story.

My mother shrugs. "From my perspective, I didn't know I was a ghost. There was nothing, and then I was aware again and at the river where I had taken my last breath. My first and only thought was *Where are my children?* I've been searching ever since."

"But they say you lure people, that you drown them on purpose."

She shakes her head sadly. "Those people of Tres Leches come here to taunt me, or they come on a dare like I'm some creature in a freak show. How cruel of them! But the anger I feel is no longer toward your father or the town. I'm angry at myself for putting my loved ones in danger. I don't call people to the river. I call for my children."

"But is it true that you put them under a spell, that they can't resist your call?"

She nods. "Yes, but I don't do that on purpose. My curse is to witness creatures drowning, and in that way, to relive my terrible mistake."

She starts to sob again, mumbling about the innocent lives, and I shudder when I remember the bones that Rooster, Ava, and I found at the bottom of the arroyo. All these years, she's been blamed. No one ever considered her point of view, that every time a creature fell into the river, she was forced to remember that horrible day. Meanwhile, my father gets to live away from it all. No one blames him, even though he's the one who pursued my mother, who went behind his wife's back to start another family. To him, I'm nothing but a child-support check and a few birthday cards. Maybe my mother's guilty, but so is my father, and so is the whole town.

"I hate my father! I hate the town! I hate what they did to you. It's not fair. *They're* the real monstruos!"

"No, mija," my mother says. "You cannot have hate in your heart." She thinks a moment. "You're right, it's not fair, but sometimes you just have to accept the way things are. If I had only accepted, your brothers would still be alive, and I would have been there for you all these years."

I shake my head, not wanting to believe that acceptance is the answer. I almost say so, but my mother shushes me.

"I have waited an eternity to speak to you," she says. "Enough of this. Tell me good things." I don't want to talk about myself, not while I'm still trying to calm down my anger, but my mother keeps prompting me. "Please, tell me about your life," she says. "And tell me about mi hermanito. I miss him so much."

When I see how eager she is, I realize she won't be able to rest until she knows that we're okay. So I tell her Uncle Clem has been taking good care of me, that he's always signing me up for things like guitar lessons, Girl Scouts, and Little Miss Kickball. I tell her about slumber parties, how my friends and I love to binge-watch romantic comedies; play light as a feather, stiff as a board; and view Instagram pics of cute boys from school. Then I bring up all the girl things I can't discuss with Uncle Clem because he gets embarrassed when I ask about my body. "That's when I've missed you the most," I say.

This whole time, my mother doesn't speak. She just listens, and with each of my stories, her face relaxes and her smile rises. All her anger and grief are slipping away, and for the first time, I see a connection between water and love because their constant flowing takes away the rough edges of stones *and* the hearts of monstruos.

I go on, telling her about my favorite ice cream, favorite teacher, favorite Christmas movie. Then I tell her about things I *don't* like—yogurt, bullies, and water, mostly water. I spend a long time on this subject since it's a big part of who I am. And the more I speak, the more youthful my mother looks. Her hands and feet are no longer twisted in pain. Her hair is soft and lustrous. Her face is without its bitter lines. Now she looks like the woman I've always imagined, the woman my uncle remembers. Beautiful and kind and happy.

But then . . . I can sense the sun coming soon because the birds and insects begin to make their morning noises.

"Mom?" I can't hide my panic because she's starting to fade. "Mom? What's happening?"

"No llores, mija. I'm at peace."

That's when I realize . . . she's going to leave me! I try reaching for her, forcing her to stay, but I can't.

"But you still have to see Uncle Clem," I say. "He loves you. He misses you. But he couldn't believe that you were alive. And now—now we can go back to town and show him. You can see him again. We can be a family!"

"We can never be together again," she says, echoing what Uncle Clem said earlier. "I died in the river, mija, and now it's time for me to rest."

"Don't go!" I cry. "I just found you."

"Remember what I said about acceptance. You need to accept that I am gone."

"But I can't. I'm supposed to bring you back with me. We're supposed to be together!"

But even as I say this, I realize that I was a fool to think I'd live with my mother from now on, that I'd have a chance to show her my report cards and drawings and photos of me growing up. Reynaldo was right when he said she was alive, but Uncle Clem was also right when he said she was dead. She drowned in that river. Then she haunted it. Now she's at peace. Now she can let go of the rage and regret that has trapped her here, and I have to let her go, even if it breaks my heart.

She's getting fainter and fainter. "Te amo, mija. Te amo mucho." Her voice is youthful and musical, no longer hoarse.

"I love you, too," I sob as she slowly fades. I gaze at her. I gaze with all my might because I want to remember every detail of her beautiful face. Then, just as the sun peeks over the horizon, my mother disappears.

BONITA! BONITA! BONITA!

FOR A LONG TIME, I stare at the spot where I last saw my mother, but it's only air now. I just sit here, stunned, trying my best to make sense of what happened. I succeeded, didn't I? I overcame my fear of water and brought my mother peace. But at what cost? She's gone, this time forever. Uncle Clem will never see her again, not even in her ghostly form. I feel horrible knowing that he missed this opportunity.

Without my mother's wails, the river's quiet, but soon I add my own cries to the morning sounds. I'm happy *and* sad, and both emotions bring tears. I freed La Llorona, and that's a happy thing, but I'll never see Alegra again, and that's sad.

I don't want to move from the spot where I last saw my mother, but then two squirrels catch my eye. They're circling a tree trunk as they chase each other. They're not Paco, but they make me think of him and my new friends—Ava, Rooster, and Reynaldo. I wouldn't have met my mother without them, especially without Reynaldo, who drove all the way to Corpus Christi to find me. Sure, his main goal was to win the election, but sometimes when you do something for yourself, you end up helping others. And now . . . now he needs *my* help. I have to find Uncle Clem, too. I have to let him know what happened.

I stand up, feeling achy and bruised from my journey down the river. One more time, I study the area, wanting to remember every detail of the place where I spent time with my mother.

"Bye, Mom." My voice cracks because it's the last thing I want to say, but I have to go, to *accept* like she said.

I follow the river upstream. Most of the time, it's an easy hike, but now and then, grasses and bushes block my way. I scratch my arms as I move the plants aside, and every step stirs up insects, mostly hungry mosquitoes. I haven't slept or eaten, so everything annoys me. "What gives you a reason to shine?" I shout to the sun, and to the flowers, "What gives you a reason to bloom?"

Finally—it must be after lunchtime—I reach the spot where I dropped my backpack. "Great," I mumble to it. "I'm already exhausted and now I have to carry you." With a bothered sigh, I slip my arms through the straps. From here, though, I know my way to Tres Leches.

When I get there, I return to the alley where I last saw Uncle Clem, eager to tell him my news, but he isn't there. He isn't anywhere. No one else is around, either. Where did everybody go?

Then I hear chanting in the distance. "Bonita! Bonita! Bonita!" There are even more VOTE FOR BONITA signs, while Reynaldo's are on the street, dirtied by footprints after being trampled. I rush toward the noise and on the way glance at the REAL-TIME POLLING RESULTS billboard. Reynaldo's ten points behind! How can this be, especially after he fulfilled his promise to make the river safe? Then again, no one knows that it was his idea to bring me, that I'm the one who's made it safe.

I follow the noise and find everyone in the town square. That's when I remember it's time for the debate. Some people are standing on picnic tables and park benches. Teenagers have climbed trees to get a better look, their legs dangling. Toddlers are perched on their parents' shoulders. I tiptoe and stretch my neck, but it's impossible to see the stage with so many before me. At least there are loudspeakers, so I can hear what's going on.

"Our town clock," a woman's voice says. She must be the moderator. "It's a major concern for our community. Mayor Reynaldo, you got it working again, but as Bonita has pointed out, it rarely shows the actual time. The town would like to know what each of you plans to do about it. Bonita, you may respond first."

"I'll make sure it gets registered as a historical landmark." Bonita's voice has a new pleasant, musical quality. "Think of it as an exhibit instead of an actual clock.

And to help all of you keep time, I will give a watch to everyone over the age of twelve." People glance at their wrists. Some have watches, but most don't. "Each morning, we'll announce the time and synchronize. Imagine it, mi gente. No more running late or running early."

I hear a grito, then a celebratory whistle followed by applause. It takes a while to die down. The moderator keeps repeating, "And now let's hear from Mayor Reynaldo."

At last, he speaks. I stand on my tiptoes, hoping to catch a glimpse of him. "Yes, yes, Bonita proposes a splendid idea. If I were smarter and more attuned to the needs of my people, I would have proposed it myself, but I just don't have the type of out-of-box thinking that would make Bonita such a wonderful mayor."

Wait a minute. *What?* Is he arguing for Bonita and against himself?

"This is ridiculous," I say out loud. Several people glance at me. "Well, it *is*!" I snap back.

I need to knock some sense into him, so I weave my way through the crowd. Instead of being polite by saying, "Excuse me," I find myself pushing people aside and saying, "Get out of my way!" and "Move over!" and "Quit being such a space hog!"

I'm finally able to glimpse the stage. The moderator is sitting in a chair, her back to the crowd. Before her are two lecterns, Reynaldo on the right and Bonita on the left, the two green-aproned men behind her. There are two flags at the back corner of the stage—the American flag and the Texas state flag. The backdrop is a black curtain.

I didn't catch the latest question because I was too busy pushing through the crowd, but Reynaldo's not talking about policy. Instead, he's pointing his piñata stick at Bonita. "Isn't she beautiful?" he's saying. "And me? I'm so flaco." He tugs at his too-short guayabera. "My clothes don't even fit. How can I be a good mayor when I can't even dress for the part?"

He continues to gush over Bonita, and I feel punched in the gut. He's so good at holding up his piñata stick and making announcements with smart vocabulary and philosophical tidbits, so I expected him to dominate the debate, to have a rebuttal for everything Bonita claimed. Instead, he keeps arguing against himself! Bonita says that planting bell peppers to fix the potholes is ridiculous, and Reynaldo says, "Quite ridiculous, the most ridiculous idea ever born." Bonita's definitely winning this debate. Then she says she'll find the kids who ran away after going to El Camarón and that she'll get rid of the mud that blocks the northern border. "It won't cost a thing," she says. "No extra taxes or fundraisers. All we have to do is settle on a trade."

Meanwhile Reynaldo claps and whistles and says,

"Very worthy causes that will greatly improve the town more than I ever did."

I try to get his attention, but he has eyes only for Bonita.

I have to find Rooster and Ava. *They'll* know how to help me. I study the crowd, looking for signs of a high pompadour or feathers, but of course my friends aren't here. They're hiding somewhere. They're *always* hiding.

I hate leaving Reynaldo, but I can't help him alone. I slip away from the crowd and search through the shadowy alleys. "Rooster, Ava, Paco!" I call, my voice echoing between the buildings.

Finally, after about ten minutes, I hear, "Felice?"

It's Rooster's voice, and then I see him stepping into view. He was crouched behind a dumpster. Ava comes out, too, and so does Paco, though he comes from *inside* the dumpster. He's got a candy wrapper and is licking the caramel that's stuck to it.

"We've been searching for you all day," Ava says. She and Rooster reach over for a group hug, but I take a step back. "Whoa!" I say. This isn't like me, but for some reason, the last thing I want is a hug.

"Are you okay?" Rooster asks.

"Yes," I say, but with a bad attitude.

"Then why are you so angry?"

"I'm *not* angry!" And I'm not. I'm really not, but my voice has its own ideas. I sniff at the air. Ugh! I can't stand how Rooster stinks. Sure, he smells the same as yesterday, but today it's just so disgusting! "Stand back!" I tell him. "You're making me gag."

"Hey!" Ava jumps in, defending her friend.

"Don't pretend like you don't want to gag, too!" I say.

"I don't!"

"That's not possible," I say. "Just like it's not possible for you to fly when you're not a bird or a bat or even a mosquito."

Paco doesn't like this one bit. He swats me with his tail.

"Watch what you're doing!" I flick his forehead.

Ava jumps between us. "Leave Paco alone!"

"I . . . I . . ." I want to say that I'm sorry, because I am, but instead, I say, "If you were a bird, Ava, you'd be an ostrich, because ostriches can't fly. And guess what, Paco, Ava's mother ate your cousins."

"Stop saying those things," Rooster insists.

"Why don't you stop dancing and get a job as an alarm clock—cock-a-doodle-do!"

Their eyes widen in shock, especially when I start repeating everything the bullies said earlier, telling Ava her mom's the only witch who doesn't need a broom and telling Rooster to go back to the sulfur pits. I can tell my insults sting, but I can't stop myself. Finally, I put my fist in my mouth to muffle my cruel words, and I plead with my eyes to let them know that I don't mean any of it.

But they don't get it. Ava says, "Come on, Rooster. Let's go. We have enough problems without adding hers to our list."

"That's right," he says, and they turn away, Paco joining them.

They can't leave. I need their help, but how can I call them back when every time I open my mouth, I say something mean?

I reach in my pocket for the magic stone. Then I hurl it in their direction, not to hit them but to get their attention. It thuds and tumbles as it hits the earth a few inches before their feet. Rooster bends down and picks it up. "A river stone," he tells Ava, and then, to me, "Where did you get this?"

I'm afraid to speak, so instead I make kissy lips. I don't care how ridiculous I look. I need them to understand that I'm under a spell.

"Bonita?" Ava guesses.

I nod.

"Why would she give you this stone?"

I mime, just like Paco, to reenact the moment I gave her my happy face emoji purse, smiling and making a heart with my fingers and framing my eyes with the shape.

"You traded your purse for it?" Ava guesses. "But why?"

I speak again. I wish I were nicer, but I can't help being

rude. "Don't you get it, morons? I needed to conquer my fear of water so I could go to the river. Bonita had that magic stone, but she would only accept a trade."

"And now," Rooster concludes, "instead of being happy, you're angry and annoyed."

"You think?" I reply with sarcasm as thick as the mud in the mud expanse.

"It's never a good idea to trade with Bonita," Rooster says. "One guy traded a goat for—"

"A stick of gum," I interrupt. "Quit changing the subject. Here's what really matters. I went to the river. I met my mother. We talked, and now that she knows I survived, she's at peace. She's not La Llorona anymore. You guys should be thanking me. The whole town should be thanking me."

"No one's going to thank you with that attitude," Ava says.

I slap my cheek, hoping to snap back to myself. "It was Reynaldo's idea, but Bonita is taking all the credit."

"We need to tell them the truth," Rooster says.

I nod. "Yes! But those fools think Bonita's sweeter than tres leches cake. Even Reynaldo's going to vote for her!"

"Hmm…" Ava cups her chin, thinking. "So we need to reverse the spell."

"Well," Rooster ventures, "we could return the stone and get back your purse."

"Duh!" I say. "Could you guys be any slower with ideas?"

Ava adjusts her tool belt. "Let's go. We need to hurry."

I nod but not without one last jab. "Who made *you* the boss?" I cover my mouth to keep from saying more, but I can't keep quiet when Paco throws a handful of dirt at me. "Hey! You little pest!" I'm about to throw dirt at *him*, but Ava stops me.

"We don't have time for this," she says. "We have to fix this before the debate ends!" She adjusts her tool belt again and starts marching toward the pharmacy.

When Rooster lifts his boom box, I tell him, "That's so last century."

I keep my mouth shut as we walk along. Since everyone's at the debate, the streets are empty. Soon, we reach the pharmacy, but of course, it's closed.

"Don't worry," Rooster says. "Paco's great at picking locks."

Sure enough, Paco straightens a paper clip and uses it to pick the lock. Once inside, we go to the aisle with remedies for los sustos. Paco picks the lock to the cabinet, and I replace the stone. Then we head to the curio cabinet, where I quickly spot my purse smiling back at me. This lock is very small, so Paco disappears for a while, returning with a couple of sewing needles. His tiny hands look like they're knitting as he makes quick adjustments. Ava puts a finger to her lips because we need to stay quiet so Paco can concentrate. I try my best, but I can't help pacing and sighing. I hold out my hands, pretending to strangle something. That's how impatient I feel.

"Let's break the glass," I say just before we hear the lock click.

Paco opens the door. The curio cabinet seems to sigh with relief, but no, it's me. I'm the one who's relieved. Instead of rushing forward, I'm frozen for a minute. Ava puts her hand on my shoulder, reminding me to relax. Then I shrug her off.

"You're still being rude," Rooster says.

"That's because the real me is in there." I nod at my purse. Without wasting another minute, I grab my purse, looping it over my shoulder.

I close my eyes and take a deep breath to reset myself. I don't feel any different, but that's okay. I didn't feel different when I first made the trade. I take a second deep breath and a third, giving the magic time to work its way through me. I tap my happy face emoji purse and give myself an emotion check. I'm still worried about Reynaldo and Uncle Clem, but I'm also glad that I'm one step closer to helping them. I don't feel irritated or angry at all.

I finally open my eyes. Rooster and Ava are looking at me, their faces full of hope and expectation, but instead of rushing into their arms for the group hug I avoided earlier, I say, "Quit staring!" and when they drop their jaws in surprise, I wave a hand in front of my nose and say, "Take a mint! Your breath reeks!"

What is wrong with me? I think it first, and then I say it: "What is wrong with me?!"

"You're still cursed," Rooster answers.

"Geez! You think?" I hold my purse in front of me, staring straight at the heart eyes. "Why am I still cursed?"

"Did Bonita give you anything else?" Ava asks.

I shake my head. "Just the stone. Am I going to be like this forever?" I glance at Rooster and Ava, hoping they can answer my question.

"When we made it rain," Ava begins, "the river came back. La Llorona came back, and the bakers got back their recipes, but they still can't bake anything sweet."

"That isn't fair," Rooster says. "They're worse off than before because we meddled with their plan."

All of us stand there, shrugging, shaking our heads, and trying our best to understand the rules of magic, and then it hits me.

"That's right!" I announce. "We meddled with the plan. I can't believe how dense we are. We brought the river back, but then we healed it—the right way!—but those tontos at the debate don't know it yet."

"But how does that help *you*?" Rooster asks.

"Maybe it doesn't, Mr. Pea Brain. Maybe I can't see the

whole picture yet, but you have to admit that it's a good observation."

Ava nods. "That's the next step, then," she says. "Time to tell the town that La Llorona's gone."

GET THAT SQUIRREL!

ROOSTER, AVA, PACO, AND I hurry back to the town square, ready to share my story, but we're too late. Bonita's already talking about the river.

"And if you remember," she's saying, "I promised to cure the river, and I delivered that promise in my role as a fellow citizen. Can you imagine how much more I can do in my role as a mayor?"

"Liar!" I shout from the back of the crowd. The people before me move aside, so I take a few steps forward. "Liar!" I shout again, and as more people step away from me, I start to run. I glance back for my friends, but they aren't there. I can't believe they're hiding again, especially when I need them the most! But there's nothing I can do about it now because the crowd is closing in behind me.

When I reach the stage, Bonita looks down at me and smiles the way you smile at a toddler who has just made a harmless mistake.

"You didn't cure the river," I explain. "*I* did. Reynaldo found me. He brought me here." I hop on the stage and turn to the crowd. "I'm the daughter of La Llorona!" The people gasp and step back.

When I glance at Bonita, she narrows her eyes. Then she turns to Reynaldo. "Did you know who she was?"

He hangs his head, ashamed. "Well . . . um . . . let me explain. . . . Okay . . . yes."

"You brought the child of un monstruo to our town?" Reynaldo nods.

"Do you see this?" Bonita asks the people. "Our mayor, who had pledged to keep us safe, brought us even more danger."

"I did," Reynaldo admits. "I don't know what I was thinking."

What happened to him? I knew he was worried about the falling poll numbers, but I never thought he'd just give up. He seemed like the type to fight, no matter how hard things got. He certainly encouraged *me* to keep fighting. And now, because of him, I've met my mother and given her peace. Because of Reynaldo, people can go to the river again. Why can't they see that?

"You were thinking of the town," I say. Then I turn to the crowd. "You dimwits, wake up! My mother was a ghost, and what do ghosts want? Come on, people! It ain't rocket science. They want peace. And what was my mother always crying for?"

"¡Sus hijos!" someone answers.

"And I'm one of those hijos. I went to her, and now that

237

she knows I'm alive, she's at peace. She won't be haunting the river anymore. And you can thank Reynaldo for that, you ungrateful rats." I slap myself, trying to hush the insults.

But Bonita's not giving up so easily. "Mi gente," she says sweetly. "Forgive me. I did not know the whole story because these two"—she points at me and Reynaldo—"they lied to me."

"It's true," Reynaldo says, "a lie of omission."

"And they're still omitting information," Bonita adds, "because this girl is leaving out a very important detail. She is afraid of water. But with my help, this child was able to face her fear and confront La Llorona. Perhaps she brought her mother peace, but only because I helped her like I have helped so many of you." At this point, she glances at me, noticing my happy face emoji purse. She shakes her head, disappointed with me but not distracted from her cause. "Without me," Bonita repeats, "she would not have had the courage to face the river and her mother. First, I dried up the river, and then I gave this girl courage. So you see, mi gente, *I* saved you from La Llorona—twice!"

At this, the crowd erupts with gritos and applause. Car horns honk. A mariachi blows his trumpet, and Reynaldo twirls his piñata stick happily.

"Don't listen to her!" I shout to the crowd. "She doesn't do anything for free. She'll take your goats and glasses and corkscrews! She'll take your happy face emoji purses!"

No one except Bonita hears me. She nods to one of the green-aproned guards, and he starts approaching. I try hopping off the stage, but he's too fast. He grabs my arm with a firm grip and leads me to the side of the stage behind a large speaker. I can still see what's happening onstage, but the crowd and I are hidden from each other.

I need to get away from the guard, but before I can formulate a plan, the moderator tells the audience to be quiet because there's a very important topic to discuss.

The crowd settles down, and the moderator returns to the debate. "Our next issue is something we've never encountered before, a new problem." Reynaldo and Bonita nod, waiting to hear more. "The town would like to know how each of you plans to deal with..." She trails off, pointing to the black curtain. We see movement behind it, and then the second green-aproned guard comes out, but he's not alone.

The crowd gasps. The "new problem" is not a problem at all—at least not in my opinion—because the thing the guard's dragging out—the *person*—is my dear uncle Clem!

He's struggling to get away, but his legs are shackled.

"Let me go!" he shouts, his voice a roar that startles people.

But the guard is too strong. There's a chair in the middle of the stage, and the guard pushes Uncle Clem onto it, handcuffing him to the armrest.

"Hey, stop being so rough!" I shout, but no one can hear me because the crowd is booing and hissing. I can't see them, but I can imagine parents covering their children's eyes and angry fists pumping the air.

I try to get his attention. "Uncle Clem! Uncle Clem!"

But he's too busy struggling to get free and shouting that he's not a monster. With all this noise and chaos, calling for him is useless. Even if I get his attention, what's next? The first guard hasn't left my side and will probably grab me if I make a sudden move. The only solution is to help Reynaldo see that the mud monstruo is really my uncle and his best friend. But how? I don't have any ideas!

Then I sniff ... and nearly gag! Sulfur!

"Psst!" I turn toward the sound. It's Rooster, Ava, and Paco peeking from behind the black curtain. When I spot them, I want to shout with joy, but Ava quickly puts a warning finger to her lips.

I'm glad they're here, but hiding behind a curtain isn't exactly helping, and I need all the help I can get because Bonita's talking again. She has a solution, while Reynaldo offers nothing.

"And to prove my abilities," Bonita's saying, "I will rid

the town of this monstruo right now." The audience and Reynaldo cheer.

"Don't listen to her!" Uncle Clem shouts. "I'm not a monster! You have nothing to fear!"

At that, Bonita nods to the guard. He pulls a rag from his apron and stuffs it in Uncle Clem's mouth, silencing him.

Bonita's attention is back on the crowd. "All I ask for," she says, "is a trade."

The moderator absentmindedly fiddles with the locket hanging from her necklace. She's not exactly offering it, but I can tell that she will. I'm sure the children would happily give up their favorite toys; the men, their best boots; and the teens, their skateboards and bikes. Bonita will make a promise and ask for a trade, and no one will think twice about giving her what she wants.

And then it begins. I hear the barber offer scissors; the members of the quilting circle, thread; and the cheerleaders, pom-poms. Bonita politely dismisses everything, and my uncle shakes his head to warn people away.

Finally, she holds out her hand, signaling them to stop making offers.

"There's only one item I'll accept in exchange for getting rid of the mud monstruo." We all hold our breath in suspense—the crowd with anticipation; Rooster, Ava, and I with dread. "I will get rid of this creature in exchange for"—Bonita looks at Reynaldo, a wicked smile crossing her face—"the mayor's piñata stick!"

Reynaldo *can't* give up his piñata stick! It's not just a stick to him. The way he holds it before giving a speech . . . It's like a lightning rod snatching inspiration from the sky.

Yet here he is. "Con mucho gusto," he says as he offers it to Bonita.

I rush forward to stop him, but of course the guard stops me, grabbing my arm again.

"Don't do it!" I shout to Reynaldo.

Finally, my uncle hears me. He *sees* me! He starts rattling the shackles and handcuffs because now he's even more desperate to get free.

I look at my friends. "Quit hiding and do something!"

At that moment, Paco jumps out, and just as Bonita reaches for the piñata stick, he intercepts, grabbing it with his teeth. Then he runs off, leaping into the crowd and using people's shoulders and heads as stepping-stones to jump across. They try to swat him, but he's too fast. Soon he's past the crowd, and I can't see where he went.

"After him!" Bonita charges. Finally, I'm free of the guard as he gives chase after Paco.

Ava panics. "He's going to catch Paco!" And she's off, running to help her friend.

"I've got an idea," Rooster says. He rushes behind the curtain again and returns with his boom box. He sets it down onstage, and hits the play button, then turns the volume to its loudest setting. Soon we hear an ensemble of violins, piano, and accordion. A tango!

I don't know what to do because I want to help my uncle *and* my friends. I have to decide, and fast. My uncle comes first. He *has* to, but he's still being guarded. I take a few steps toward him, but he warns me off with his eyes. He nods toward the crowd, ordering me to follow my friends and to keep the piñata stick away from Bonita.

All of this is happening in an instant, and it's a good thing, too, because Bonita has just remembered me and is telling the guard to secure me.

"I'll be back!" I tell Uncle Clem as I jump off the stage, barely escaping.

The first chance I get, I snatch a baseball cap off a boy's head. He's too distracted by the commotion to notice. Then I spot a rebozo that's fallen on the ground and wrap the dirty thing around my shoulders. I don't like taking things that aren't mine, but I need a quick disguise because everyone knows that I'm La Llorona's daughter.

It's hard to see Rooster because so many people are taller than me. I decide to sniff the air to follow his scent. It works! I can definitely smell those rotten eggs.

243

Finally, I find him just as he reaches the green-aproned man who is inches from Ava and Paco!

I'm ready to lunge and grab the man by his apron, but before I can do anything, Rooster taps the man's shoulder and asks, "May I have this dance?"

His magic works! The man can't refuse. He and Rooster get into a dancers' hold and start to tango. Because of Rooster's smell, people stand back, clearing a circle for them. I crane my neck, searching for Ava and Paco, but they're no longer in sight. Hopefully they're far away by now.

Rooster and the guard continue to dance, their rhythm a pattern of slow-slow, quick-quick, slow steps. They move in circles and figure eights. They do sharp scissors kicks and even sharper turns. At one point, Rooster dips the man, stopping a few inches above the ground.

"Go help him!" we hear Bonita say to the other green-aproned guard.

He hops off the stage and approaches. It's up to me to stop him. I run right up to him to block his path, but he's like a football player, tackling me aside. I quickly stand up again and give chase. I'll jump on his back if I have to! But I don't get a chance. He's already reached his partner and is grabbing his arm to steer him away, but luckily he doesn't get far. Rooster asks *him* to dance, too, so now my friend is doing the tango with both men, pulling one closer while pushing the other away and somehow circling back again.

A woman is holding a bouquet of wildflowers. Rooster plucks one from her and tucks it behind the first man's ear. Then he grabs another flower and tucks it behind the second man's ear. I'm so impressed by Rooster's ability to lead the men in this very beautiful dance.

The music abruptly stops, and the men shake their heads as if awakening from a strange dream. We all glance at the stage. Bonita's opening the boom box and removing the CD. She holds it up for all to see, then snaps it in half.

"Get that squirrel!" she orders, pointing an angry finger at the green aprons.

They take off. There's no stopping them now.

WHAT ELSE MAKES YOU SHIVER?

ROOSTER LOOKS TOWARD THE green-aproned men while I look toward the stage.

"I need to help my uncle," I say.

"Don't worry," he assures me. "Ava and I will make sure they don't get their hands on that piñata stick."

He takes off, but once the odor dissipates, the crowd closes in again. I have to elbow my way back to the stage. It's not easy. The people seem more tightly packed now. I come face-to-face with some of them, but the cap and rebozo prove a good disguise. Besides, everyone's focusing on Bonita again.

I continue to make my way through the crowd while Reynaldo offers more trades. "You may have the piñata stick when it's recovered, but in the meantime, if I may offer an alternative, how about my guayabera?" He starts unbuttoning his shirt. Bonita shakes her head. "My mayoral buckle, then?" He starts unclasping his buckle, but this time, Bonita refuses by crossing her arms. "Perhaps you would appreciate the keys to my monster truck, for there is no better way to chase away monstruos than in a truck named after the most fright-ening: El Cucuy."

"No shirt, no buckle, no truck," Bonita says. "I want the piñata stick, and I want it now." She sounds evil. Surely everyone hears it, but no, they're still on her side.

"Of course you do," Reynaldo says apologetically. "How foolish of me to think that anything else would suffice."

Bonita turns to the crowd. "If I don't have that piñata stick in the next five minutes, I will release this mud monstruo. Then we'll see how truly dangerous he is, and it'll be *Reynaldo's* fault."

My uncle tries to defend himself, but he's still shack-led and gagged.

"Move aside!" I say, pushing my way through the crowd and trying as hard as I can to reach him. The rebozo gets caught on someone's buckle and slips off, so I dip the brim of the hat to cast a shadow over my face.

Meanwhile, instead of being angry at Bonita for her threat, the crowd is angry at Reynaldo, booing and hiss-ing at him. Someone throws a crushed soda can at the stage, and it lands at his feet. Someone else throws a half-eaten burrito at my uncle. It plops against his leg and rolls off.

"I take full responsibility," Reynaldo says, "for what-ever fear this monstruo has caused in the past, is caus-ing in the present, and will cause in the future. I will pay for the damages with my money, my possessions, and my title as mayor."

That's it. I can't take it anymore. I make a final lunge through the crowd and jump onto the stage once again. A gust of wind frees the baseball cap.

"Stop!" I cry. "Do not make that trade!"

Before Reynaldo can respond, a woman cries out. "It's that girl! It's the daughter of La Llorona!"

She has fear in her voice, but a teenager has a different reaction.

"I'm not afraid of monstruos!" he shouts as he reaches into his back pocket to pull out a gun. He points it at me. I can't believe it. This boy doesn't even know me, yet he's going to pull the trigger!

Uncle Clem is finally able to spit out the gag. "Don't hurt her!"

I panic, imagining a bullet, but no, it's *worse* than a bullet. The boy doesn't have a real gun, but a *water* gun! When the cold squirt hits my arm, I jump back, afraid. He laughs and squirts me again. This time, the bones and muscles in my legs abandon me, and I fall to my knees, one hand at my throat because it's tight and I can hardly breathe. I don't understand. I was in the river all last night. Why am I freaking out *now*, when I'm not in danger of drowning? Then I remember. I no longer have the stone.

"Damas y caballeros," Bonita says, the noisy audience

248

hushing to hear her message. "I was speaking la verdad." She points at me. "Look at her. She has a susto, and the thing she fears the most is water. Yes, she brought her mother peace, but only because *I* gave her the courage." She shakes her head with sympathy, but I can tell it's fake. "Now she cowers again, la pobrecita."

"Leave her alone!" Uncle Clem shouts, but he's still covered in mud and no one recognizes his voice. Instead, the audience is muttering about me. They saw me with Ava and Rooster. They know I'm the daughter of La Llorona. And now this new monstruo is trying to defend me, so they've decided that I must be a monstruo, too. I hear Uncle Clem's voice asking me if I'm okay, but I can only tremble in response.

Just then the green-aproned men return. They're holding the piñata stick, one man on each side and Paco in the middle, dangling because he's still clenching the stick with his teeth and won't let go. They offer the stick to Bonita.

She shakes her head. "This is Reynaldo's to give."

They return the stick to Reynaldo, who swings it as if hitting an invisible piñata. Paco finally loses his grip, skidding to a stop beside me. He looks at me, questioning. "I . . . I . . ." I can't say another word because I'm still coping with my fear.

Reynaldo holds up the piñata stick for one more speech before giving it away. "It is with great pleasure and with a sense of duty to my community and to . . ."

I can't listen anymore. My whole world is shutting down. Once Reynaldo gives up the piñata stick, Bonita is sure to win the election. But the worst part is seeing my uncle handcuffed to a chair and the fear in his eyes because he's worried about me.

". . . symbol of authority and responsibility fashioned by my own hands," Reynaldo goes on.

I want to help my uncle, but I'm too afraid, not because of the people but because I'm still wet. So now I'm shackled like my uncle, not by iron but by water. Bonita's right. I couldn't get near the river before she gave me the stone.

Wait a minute. The stone . . . it let me face my fear, yes, but . . . I never *overcame* my fear. I think about Lulu, who traded her corkscrew for a whistle because she hadn't learned how to listen *and* how to be heard. I think about the cartographer, who traded his glasses for an eraser because for some reason, he's afraid to explore beyond the county lines. And I think of the town, the bakers, how everyone just wants to get rid of La Llorona without accepting their role in her curse. To break a curse, you have to change something inside yourself, which means that I have to face water without a magic item for protection.

"Paco," I whisper to my friend. "Go tell Ava to open

the fire hydrant with her tools. I need water. Lots and lots of water."

Paco gives me a salute and runs off.

"And so," Reynaldo says, "after much pontification—but not deliberation, for who needs to deliberate when the right course of action is before us?—I offer Bonita—"

"No!" I shout, finding the courage and strength to stand and block his offering. "You can't do this."

"Oh, but I must."

My knees are still trembling, but like a dog, I shake off the remaining water. Then, before Reynaldo can reach Bonita, I grab the stick, holding him back. He doesn't give in. He has one end, and I have the other.

"Felice, be careful!" Uncle Clem calls.

I can't afford to be careful, not if it means Bonita gets the stick.

Reynaldo and I are in a game of tug-of-war, and as we fight it out, the crepe paper tears away, revealing the broomstick beneath. I readjust my hands as we go back and forth with our pulling. My grip is strong, but Reynaldo's is stronger. I feel the stick slipping away. I'm going to lose my grip and so much more, and then—

Water! My friends have succeeded, and just in time. They've attached a hose to the fire hydrant and are pointing it at the sky right above the stage, making it rain upon us. The first thing I do is release the piñata stick to cover my face as I cower. Luckily, the water has distracted everyone. They've forgotten about the piñata stick and my uncle as they shield themselves by opening umbrellas, hiding beneath ponchos, or lifting campaign signs above their heads.

I can't worry about what they're doing because I'm too worried about myself. I'm getting even wetter!

I want to run away, but then I remember . . . I must face my fear. If not for myself, then for my uncle, for Reynaldo, and for the town. The water is pelting me, a hundred fingers flicking my shoulders and back, but I ask myself . . . does it hurt? And the answer is no, not really. Sure, it's uncomfortable, but it isn't painful. I'm not going to get bruises or need stitches after being hit by these droplets. I let this new thought settle in. For the first time, I take a breath while standing in a down-pour. It's not an easy breath, but it's a start. At least I'm not hyperventilating. But remembering to breathe isn't enough because I'm still shivering from fear.

"I want to be brave," I say, looking to my uncle, "but I can't stop shivering!"

"What else makes you shiver?" he asks me.

It seems like a strange question until I remember his strategies for helping me cope with fear. What sounds like rain but isn't scary? Popcorn. Where else have I shivered? The cartographer's shop! It was so cold in there. That's the answer. Yes! This water is cold! *Maybe*

I'm shivering because I'm afraid, or maybe I'm just cold. The thought makes me stand a little straighter, and as I do, I catch Reynaldo looking at his piñata stick with confusion. He doesn't seem so eager to give it away anymore.

I haven't run away yet, and I'm still breathing, a little more easily now. This is probably the longest I've ever stood in any kind of rain, but I still need to face my fear, and I mean literally face it.

I make sure my feet are firmly planted on the ground. They are, but my knees are still shaking, and my heart is still thumping hard against my chest. Every muscle wants to run, but I have to break this curse.

I close my eyes. Inch by tiny inch, I lift my chin, tilting my head back farther and farther. The drops are now pelting my face, but I remind myself that it doesn't hurt and that I'm shivering because the water's cold. And then . . . I open my eyes to the blue sky and all that water, and I open my mouth, letting the drops fall in. Nothing bad happens. I'm not drowning! I'm not going to drown!

I laugh and then I lift my arms to give a giant hug to the water. I start to spin because now the cheery songs like "Raindrops Keep Fallin' on My Head" and "Singin' in the Rain" make sense. They finally make sense!

"I refuse to be afraid!" I shout to the sky. "I am *not* afraid!" Then I look for Rooster, Ava, and Paco, and when I find them, still with the water hose, I point and say, "You guys are the best friends a girl could ask for!"

And that's when I know the curse is broken, because I'm being kind again and because Reynaldo isn't confused anymore. He's got a protective hold on his piñata stick. No way is he giving it up now.

I run back to my uncle and kneel before him. The water's landing on him, too. He's still covered in mud, but slowly, it's washing away.

"I'm sorry I ran away from you, but I had to meet my mother. And I did. I met her. You were right. She was a ghost. An angry, terrifying ghost."

He winces. "Did she try to hurt you, mija?"

"No. I fell into the river, and she tried to rescue me, but she couldn't because her hands . . ." I look at my own for a second. "Her hands just went through me."

"How did you get out?"

"I remembered what you said about helping myself first, so I figured out how to swim to the riverbank." He nods and smiles at this. "And somehow, I rescued Mom, too. We talked—about *everything*. I thought she'd join us after I found her. I thought she'd be with us forever. But once she found peace, she disappeared."

This whole time, I'm only vaguely aware of what's happening behind me, but it sounds like Reynaldo and Bonita are in a heated debate. He isn't gushing anymore. He's arguing his points now that the spell is broken, but when I glance back, the people are lining up with their offerings. They still think there's un monstruo on the stage even though I'm starting to see Uncle Clem's skin beneath the mud.

"I didn't want Mom to disappear," I continue, "but it's a good thing, I guess, because she's resting now. I mean, I wish she were here—not as a ghost but as a flesh-and-blood person. My brothers, too. And I'll probably be wishing for that my whole life. But at least I have a memory now, my own memory. Maybe our time together was short, but I'll take a few minutes over nothing at all. And, Uncle Clem?"

"Yes?"

"She wants me to thank you for taking care of me all these years. She wants you to know that she loves you, that you should be proud. She knows you were there for her."

A drop rolls across the mud on his face. I know it's from a tear and not from the fire hydrant. I reach over to wipe it, and some of the mud comes off. Then I wipe his shoulder and more mud comes off.

"Uncle Clem. The mud. It's finally washing away."

He lifts his face to the rain. It's all he can do, since he's strapped to the chair.

"All these years," he says, "I blamed myself for what happened to your mother and brothers. I never let myself relax because every minute of every day, I worried something bad was going to happen to you, and that I'd get there too late, just like I was too late for our family." He laughs. "Turns out, you can take care of yourself."

"I had a good teacher," I say, hugging him.

Before we can say more, the downpour stops, and when I glance in the direction of the fire hydrant, I see the green-aproned men. They've run my friends away and shut off the valve.

"And now," Bonita says, turning to Reynaldo as she wrings water from the hem of her lab coat, "the piñata stick."

Instead of approaching her, Reynaldo takes a step back.

She narrows her eyes at him. Streaks of mascara are like black claws on her cheeks, and the heart on her lips has washed away.

Reynaldo tightens his grip on the stick. "I will not trade with you."

"No matter," she says before turning her attention back to the crowd. "Mi gente, I will now accept your offerings to rid you of this monstruo."

A few move forward, but when they look up, they stop. Someone points and shouts, "He's not a monstruo anymore!" and someone else says, "Hey, it's our old cracksman!"

Reynaldo looks, too. "Clemente? Is that you?"

The crowd starts muttering as they take in this

news. I hear "cascarones" and "Clemente." They recognize him and seem happy he's back.

"Yes, it's me," my uncle says to his friend. "I came to rescue Felice, but it looks like she's the one who rescued me."

"There was never a monstruo," someone observes, loud enough for everyone to hear. "It's just Clemente. He's come back. Bonita was trying to fool us to win the election!"

"I was not!" she protests, but no one seems to believe her.

Meanwhile, Paco jumps on the stage. He's stolen the keys from one of the guards and is using them to free my uncle. As soon as my uncle stands, Reynaldo grabs him for un abrazo fuerte.

Meanwhile, the people have turned away from the stage, gathering in small groups to chat about this new development. I hear them mentioning piñatas, piggy banks, and crispy taco shells. The children's eyes are wide with amazement, and I realize that many have never seen the wondrous things that a cracksman makes. With all this excitement, the town has forgotten about Bonita, and she's not happy about it, especially because the REAL-TIME POLLING RESULTS billboard shows her popularity sinking. She's still ahead, but not for long.

She points at me and my uncle and shouts to her

green-aproned guards. "Take them away! They have no business here! They aren't citizens of Tres Leches!"

The guards approach, but Reynaldo blocks them. "I'm still the mayor, still in charge." He calls for a few police officers who've been patrolling the crowd but ignoring the commotion because they were under Bonita's spell. "Escort these men off the stage, and if they refuse to leave, arrest them."

Bonita glares at the green-aproned men, her eyes ordering them to stay. It's no use. They don't want to go to jail. They may be big, strong, and good employees, but they're not unconditionally loyal anymore.

No one is. The line for offerings is gone. There's no monstruo, so no need to make a trade. But Bonita isn't giving up. She points at random people. "You, you, and you. Get back in line." They shake their heads, refusing.

Then she looks at the billboard again. Reynaldo has caught up! They're tied! And . . . suddenly she's a point behind!

"Ugh!" Bonita shouts. "You people are never here for me. You are more than happy to accept my help when you're in trouble, but when *I* need *you*–" She stops because no one's listening. They've forgotten about Bonita because they're too excited about my uncle's return. "When I need you," Bonita repeats in a whisper, "you turn away."

I feel sorry for her, remembering what Reynaldo said

about her lack of friends and how she once helped others for free, but my pity doesn't last long because she
quickly gets over her disappointment and narrows her
eyes at the crowd. "Malagradecidos!" she spits out. Then
she stomps off, popping the balloons and tearing at the
ribbons that decorate the stage.

SHE WANTED FLAMINGOS

THERE'S A LOT OF noise after Bonita leaves, but when the crowd settles down, Reynaldo speaks to them again.

"My friends," he says. "I promised to make the river safe, and knowing that ghosts will never truly leave until they find peace, I went in search of La Llorona's daughter." He beckons my uncle and me, so we go stand beside him. "She's been living in Corpus Christi with her uncle, our cracksman, but she made this journey to meet her mother and rid this town of La Llorona's curse."

"That's right," I say. "My mother stopped haunting the river early this morning, and even though"—I take a second to gather myself—"even though I will never see her again, I'm glad she's at peace."

The people turn to each other to discuss this news. They cup their hands and whisper in each other's ears, not wanting us to know what they're saying.

Finally, a baker speaks up. "You say she left this morning?"

"Yes," I answer. "At sunrise."

He squints as if doubting me. "Are you sure? Because I tried to make empanadas, but they burned in the oven."

"And my marranitos," another baker adds, "they are all headless!"

"We gave our recipes to Bonita," the first baker says, "but then we got them back when the river returned. If it's no longer cursed, why are we still unable to make our pan dulce?"

Everyone starts accusing us—some calling us liars, others calling us frauds. Fists pump in the air, and a few people stomp in protest. Reynaldo tries to calm them down, saying, "Order! Order!"

I can only shake my head as I try to figure things out. Why are their recipes failing? I glance toward the fire hydrant, searching for support from my friends, but a few townspeople have discovered them and are shooing them away. I see one woman holding her nose. Bonita was right about one thing. These people are malagradecidos. Don't they know that Rooster and Ava have helped them? How can Reynaldo call this the sweetest place in Tejas when—

Wait a minute . . . the sweetest . . . pan dulce . . . pan dulce is *sweet* bread.

"You don't deserve your pan dulce!" I say, shouting to get their attention. "How can you make sweet bread when you have nothing but bitterness in your hearts?"

And now Uncle Clem finally addresses the crowd.

261

"What she says is true," he begins. "My sister made a mistake by falling in love with a married man who left her to raise three children alone, but instead of helping her, comforting her, you turned your backs. You gossiped. You stopped inviting her to your get-togethers and hiring her for your events right when she really needed the money."

A couple of people hang their heads, ashamed, but most are still complaining.

"Order! Order!" Reynaldo demands again, and when no one listens, he pounds the piñata stick on the stage, three sharp thuds. This finally gets their attention.

"Go on," Reynaldo urges my uncle.

"Mr. Rivera," Uncle Clem says to a man in a cowboy hat, "when you were getting married, you told my sister that you didn't want to drive off in a car with strings of cans like everybody else. Do you remember what my sister did for you?"

Mr. Rivera smiles. "She found us a hot-air balloon with wind chimes dangling off the sides."

Several people look to the sky as if remembering.

"It made beautiful music as it floated away," Mr. Rivera adds.

"And you, Ms. Luna." Uncle Clem nods to a woman with a VOTE FOR BONITA T-shirt. "When your daughter had her quinceañera, she didn't want boys to escort the damas, remember?"

Ms. Luna chuckles. "She wanted flamingos."

Everybody laughs at this.

"But Alegra never said my daughter was unreasonable," Ms. Luna adds.

"It wasn't easy," Uncle Clem says, "but Alegra found fourteen flamingos, put bow ties around their necks, and managed to get them to walk in a straight line for the procession."

"You had to see it with your own eyes," someone says, which makes a bunch of people search their phones for the pictures.

"My mother did that?" I ask my uncle because I've never heard these stories. These are exactly the types of memories I've always wanted.

"She brought a lot of joy to this community," Uncle Clem says, both to me and to the crowd.

There's a moment of silence as everyone remembers. Then a man steps forward. "Oye, amigo, you brought us joy, too." Several people nod in agreement. "We miss you, Clemente," he says.

"Will you come back?" a woman asks, and so many others chime in, saying they miss his piñatas and crispy taco shells.

Uncle Clem takes a long time to answer. He's spent so many years running away, so many years angry. As well as I know my uncle, I can't predict what he'll say. The crowd waits expectantly. Reynaldo puts a hand on his shoulder. "Tres Leches is your home," he says.

Uncle Clem nods, then looks at me as if asking for permission.

"It should be my home, too," I say.

He takes another long moment, and at last, he turns to the crowd. "I've missed you, too, my friends, but things will have to change. My sister was hurt by your gossip, by the way you enjoyed talking behind her back."

The people hang their heads again with renewed shame.

"That's the bitterness I was talking about," I say. "Even now, you turn away my friends, Rooster and Ava." I look in the direction where I last saw them, but only Paco is there. "I didn't work alone."

"Mayor Reynaldo helped you," someone confirms.

"Yes, but so did Rooster and Ava. They were with me every step of the way. They wanted to help the town even after all your cruel words."

There's a long moment of silence and more downcast eyes.

Then a woman speaks up. "My name is Ms. Cavasos, and I am the principal of the school. It . . . it's . . ." She takes a deep breath as if to gather courage. "It is my responsibility to protect the children, all of them, including Ava and Rooster, but I have not done a very good job. For that, I am truly sorry. From now on," she says, her voice loud and confident, "they will be welcome at our school."

"And at our bakeries!" someone adds.

"And all our tienditas!"

One by one and then all at once, the townspeople promise to change. I glance at Paco, give him the signal to get Ava and Rooster, and a few minutes later, they emerge from the shadows. Uncle Clem and Reynaldo join me in urging my friends onto the stage. When the people see them, they cheer. Some whistle. Others let out their gritos. Several kids blow through their kazoos, and amid all this happiness, a viejita makes her way to the stage. She's suddenly before me, leaning heavily on her cane and panting after climbing the stairs. She takes my hands, and the crowd hushes out of respect for her.

When she catches her breath, she says, "Mija." Her gravelly tone reminds me of my mother's voice when she was still La Llorona. "Because of us, you have grown up without a mother and without brothers, but we promise you"—she looks to crowd, and everyone is nodding—"we promise . . . you will always be welcome here. Can you forgive us? Can you . . . *accept* us?"

"Yes," I say with no hesitation. And then I'm una llorona again, my tears and the emotions behind them reminding me of something Reynaldo said back at the restaurant in Corpus Christi—how we cry for sorrow but also for joy.

The viejita embraces me. Even though I'm hugging only one person, I understand that I'm really hugging the whole town. And when we finally move apart, I look to Rooster, Ava, and Paco, finally giving them the group hug I'd avoided earlier.

As the town celebrates, Reynaldo gains points on the REAL-TIME POLLING RESULTS billboard, and once Uncle Clem and I are confident that he'll win tomorrow's election, we sneak away from the crowd.

"Let's go to the river," he suggests.

I take him there, and as soon as I hear the rushing water, my heart races and my knees tremble. It's going to take me a while to completely overcome my anxiety, but at least I'm not letting my fear keep me from my destination.

When we get to the river, Uncle Clem kneels beside the water. I join him. I thought coming here would bring back his memories of that terrible night, but when I glance at him, he seems peaceful, just like my mother this morning. I lean over to see my reflection, and in the play of light and ripples, I find my mother's face instead of my own. I smile, and she smiles back. I wave, and she waves back. I blink a few times, and now I see myself again. Of course it was always me in the water. But maybe not. Maybe my mother is still here, not as a cursed ghost but as a guardian angel. I touch the water, swirling it, the reflection twisting this way and that. When the image returns, I see both me and my mother staring back.

EPILOGUE

ALL THE STUDENTS OF Tres Leches, their teachers, parents, the bakers, the city council, Mayor Reynaldo Martínez de la Peña, Clem the cracksman, and Felice make their way to the new La Llorona Park. Some people are carrying picnic baskets, and others badminton racquets or horseshoes. The cracksman, of course, is carrying a piñata shaped like a giant slice of tres leches cake.

"Hey, Clemente!" A man pats the cracksman on his back. "It's been a while."

"Too long," Clem agrees.

Then the man starts laughing. "Remember that time we let some air out of the basketballs? Not enough to make them flat but enough to deaden the bounce? Watching those guys try to dribble was so funny."

"Too bad we got caught," Clem says.

"Pues we had a good hiding spot beneath the bleachers, but then you let out that loud pedo."

Everybody laughs about the fart.

"You know why your uncle became the cracksman?"

the man asks Felice. She shakes her head. "Because he was always cracking us up with his pranks!"

Clem and the man share a few more memories as they walk along, but then Lulu interrupts them with her whistle.

"We've got a lot of catching up to do," she tells Clem. "Might as well start at the beginning. The day you left was a Thursday, remember? Did you know Thursday was originally known as Thor's Day? Now, this Thor was an ancient Norse god. Seems like all those ancient people liked to name things after their gods. Take the planet Mars, which was the name for the Roman god of war. And Jupiter was named after the king of the gods, since it's the biggest planet. Just a tad bigger and it would have been a second sun. And don't get me started on the constellations."

They don't, but she talks anyway, moving from the names of constellations to the big bang theory to the primordial soup where life began.

"Oh, look. There's Suzanne," Lulu says. "I haven't talked to her in ages." She rushes ahead. "Suzanne! Suzanne!" Her friend turns around, but when she sees Lulu, she speeds up, trying to get away. Lulu doesn't notice. She just blows her whistle and speeds up, too.

The group finally reaches the clearing before the river, the same clearing where the BEWARE THE RIVER sign once stood. Picnic tables are scattered about.

There's a volleyball net and a pole for tetherball, and the teenagers rush to play both. A barbecue pit fills the air with the delicious aroma of fajitas. Giant glass jugs of aguas frescas are lined up on a table—agua de jamaica, agua de sandía, and lemonade. A boy waves a wand to make bubbles, and his dog snaps at them. A mariachi band is tuning up in the new gazebo, where a couple of women are tying a red ribbon between the posts.

The old wooden sign has been removed, and in its place is a marble stone with a bronze plaque that says:

LA LLORONA PARK,
DEDICATED IN LOVING MEMORY TO
ALEGRA, GUSTAVO, AND HENRY.
MAY THEY REST IN PEACE.

This is Mayor Reynaldo's first act during his second term as mayor, honoring the memory of Alegra and her sons with this park. Now when people come here, they'll remember the sad story and all the years the river was haunted, but hopefully they'll also remember to be kind and supportive when people make mistakes.

Felice and her uncle stand before the new sign. They're silent, admiring their family's memorial. Felice kisses her fingers and touches them to the names of her mother and brothers. Her uncle Clem does the same.

And then someone taps a microphone, the staticky

269

sound alerting everyone. They all head to the gazebo, including the cartographer.

"As if I didn't have enough to do," he's saying. "Now there's this park. Did anyone bother to send me the dimensions? No. I have to calculate them myself."

He's got a ruler, not the kind for land surveys but a twelve-inch ruler. He places it on the ground and draws a slash in a little notebook he's carrying, determined to measure the space one foot at a time.

"Testing, testing, one-two-three." It's Mayor Reynaldo, standing in the gazebo before the microphone.

"Coming through, loud and clear," a technician says.

"Good. Very, very good." Reynaldo claps his hands. "Let's get this show on the road!" he announces.

The teens stop their volleyball and tetherball games. The people at the barbecue pit stay put but turn their attention to the mayor. Even Lulu hushes to listen.

Reynaldo closes his eyes a moment and holds up the piñata stick as he prepares to make a speech. Then he's ready. He leans toward the microphone and begins. "Four score and seven years ago." He chuckles to himself. "I don't know what *four score* means," he admits, "but it worked for President Lincoln, so I figure it'll work for me, too." He clears his throat, gets serious again. "I have a dream. The longest journey begins with a single step. A *small* step. One small step for man, one giant step for mankind. New worlds and new civilizations. Let's boldly go where no one has gone before. And let's . . . let's . . . let's ask not what your town can do for you but what you can do for your town. And in the spirit of doing something for the town, we have created this new park, dedicating it to the memory of our beloved Alegra, Gustavo, and Henry, who tragically drowned here twelve years ago." He pauses and in a solemn voice says, "Let's have a moment of silence."

He lowers his head and closes his eyes. Everyone follows his example, and since no one's looking, Rooster, Ava, and Paco come out of hiding—for they are still cautious around the townspeople even though everyone has apologized a dozen times. Rooster takes one of Felice's hands while Ava takes her other hand and Paco hugs her ankle. Felice's smile is as wide as the one on her happy face emoji purse.

Then the moment of silence is over.

"The river was banned for many years," Reynaldo continues. "But fear not, for now that La Llorona is at peace, we have nothing to fear but fear itself. Remember . . . fortune favors the bold. And *also* remember"—he rubs his stomach and pats his heart—"panza llena, corazón contento. *Full stomach, happy heart*—it's the most popular dicho in our town, once again the sweetest place in Tejas. And now . . ." He sets down his piñata stick to grab a pair of scissors, opening the blades and letting them *stay* open to increase the suspense before finally, in a dramatic move, snapping them shut to cut the ribbon. "The festivities may commence!" he cheers. "Or, to put it more simply but just as fervently—let's party!"

At that, the mariachi band strikes its first chord, and they play "Las mañanitas." It's mostly played for birthdays, but it works here, too. Besides, this *is* a birthday—a birthday for the park.

The crowd disperses, some returning to their games and others to the picnic tables. Rooster, Ava, and Paco start dancing, big smiles on their faces as others join in. Most of the children run to a tree where Clem the cracksman is hoisting the piñata. This is the first time they've played this game and each of them begs to go first. Mayor Reynaldo chooses a boy, blindfolds him, then spins him a few times before handing over the piñata stick, the *mayor's* piñata stick. Perhaps all along, this is what he had hoped for when he made it.

The boy gets ready to swing, holding the stick like a bat. Just as he's about to strike, Clem pulls on the rope, lifting the piñata. The stick swooshes through the air. The boy gets two more tries but strikes out. Then it's a girl's turn. Her first swing misses, too.

"¡A la izquierda!" someone calls.

She strikes to the left but misses again. Then she starts flailing wildly, aiming in all directions till finally making contact. There's a crack and then another. Now that there's a hole in the piñata, Clem makes it swing by lifting and lowering the rope. Tootsie Rolls, lollipops, and bubble gum rain down. He laughs and laughs as the children shove one another playfully and stuff their pockets with candy.

But Felice has wandered off by herself. Today is for the river. When she gets there, a viejita fishing upstream waves and shouts, "Welcome to the river!" She casts her line back and forth, letting the feathered hook lightly tap the surface to fool the fish into thinking it's an insect.

Felice walks along the bank till she reaches a pile of inner tubes. They're from old trucks. Some have patches from previous flats, and all have long metal valves that attach to compressors. Even now, a man is filling them with air.

She removes her tank top and shorts to reveal her new bathing suit. Then she grabs an inner tube and steps into the river, going knee-deep. The water's cool, the perfect answer to this hot day. She looks at her reflection and smiles. She whispers, "Hello, Mom."

When she tries to settle onto the inner tube, she flips over a few times, laughing at her own clumsiness. Luckily, the water's not deep, and there are plenty of people nearby if she needs help. She finally manages to climb on, her legs and arms dangling off the sides. Now she's floating down the river, occasionally splashing the water.

She doesn't know where the river is taking her or where she'll be when she gets out. The river, the way the current rocks her—up and down, back and forth—it's as gentle and loving as a mother's arms.

AUTHOR'S NOTE

EACH SUMMER, THE MARTÍNEZ family drove to the Hill Country of Texas to camp at Garner State Park. My cousins and I loved playing in the Rio Frio, the water always ice-cold just as its name suggests. We loved renting pedal boats or swinging from a rope to splash into the river. Our favorite activity was tubing. My father and uncles would drive us upstream and drop us off. We'd get comfy in our inner tubes, the river carrying us lazily along. Sometimes, we enjoyed the thrill of mild rapids. Sometimes, the water was too shallow, so we had to portage our tubes.

We were at ease in the river, and perhaps that's why our parents chose this location to tell us the story of La Llorona. In their version, she was a ghost who came out at night and prowled the riverbanks, searching for children and drowning any who came near. They'd ask us to listen. Perhaps it was our imaginations, but we often heard La Llorona's cries. "If you go to the river," our folks would say, "La Llorona will get you!"

She was always a threat, an evil monstruo.

Later, I would hear a more developed story. La Llorona was a peasant woman who married a wealthy man (in some versions, she is an Indigenous woman of Mexico and he is the colonizer). She drowned her children when her husband left her for someone else. Sometimes, she was his mistress, not his wife. Sometimes, she seduced him. But in all versions, the man leaves her, and she drowns her own children in an act of rage. She is always to blame, and often not only for drowning her children but for thinking that she could rise above her station and be worthy of a man from the wealthy class.

Like many who've heard this legend, I blamed her at first, too. But then I started to ask questions. Where were her friends? Where was her family? Didn't she have a support system, someone beyond the man who betrayed her? And why was he never to blame? And the best story-starter of them all, the "what if" question: What if La Llorona wasn't a monster, but a loving mother who temporarily lost her way, and what if one of her children survived? With these questions in mind, I started this story, hoping to give La Llorona and her children the peace they deserve.

ACKNOWLEDGMENTS

I AM SO GRATEFUL for all the people who have guided me and been my companions on this writing journey. Thanks to my agent and friend, Stefanie Sanchez Von Borstel, who has been with me since day one on this and many other projects. I could not have asked for a better person to help me find homes for my books. You are the best, Stefanie!

Also, much gratitude for Joanna Cárdenas, whose insights helped me realize this story's full potential, and for the Kokila team, whose great questions guided me in the revision process. Your insights really challenged me to think more deeply about the story and how it "talks" to other stories and representations of La Llorona. Thanks to Pablo Leon for his fabulous artwork and the ability to capture the adventurous spirit of this book. I'd also like to thank the landscape of South Texas, in particular the strip of 285 between Riviera and Falfurrias. My drives along that road informed my vision of the fictional town Tres Leches.

Sometimes, it helps to have an audience when I think aloud, so I'd like to thank the patient listeners in my life: dear friends Vanesa Sanabria and Saba Razvi;

my parents, Albert and Patricia Martínez; my loving husband, Gene López; and my fur babies, Birdy, Bella, and Benji, who don't understand me but listen just the same. This book is dedicated to my nephews, Steban, Seth, and Deven. They are young men now, but I'm so happy to have seen them grow up. My time and chats with them have been a great source of inspiration and have kept me close to the magic of childhood.